A Note to Readers

While the Allertons and their friends are fictional, the Easter riots actually took place. After the Civil War, there was increasing tension between people who owned companies and the people who worked for them. Some owners did not care if their employees were working in dangerous places. They refused to pay their workers enough money to live on.

Because of these problems, workers formed unions. They thought if they worked together against company owners, they would have a better chance of getting more pay and safer working conditions. Sometimes they were successful. Many times they were not. And too often, violence erupted.

In most places, unions weren't legal. Sometimes company owners paid people to break up the unions. Many union members were killed, and some union members killed company supporters in return. This conflict went on for decades. It wasn't until 1935 that the federal government passed a law guaranteeing workers the right to form unions.

☆ The ☆
STREETCAR
RIOTS

Susan Martins Miller

BARBOUR
PUBLISHING, INC.
Uhrichsville, Ohio

© MCMXCVIII by Barbour Publishing, Inc.

ISBN 1-57748-290-5

Published by Barbour Publishing, Inc.
    P.O. Box 719
    Uhrichsville, Ohio 44683
    http://www.barbourbooks.com

 Member of the
Evangelical Christian
Publishers Association

Printed in the United States of America.

Cover illustration by Peter Pagano.
Inside illustrations by Adam Wallenta.

Chapter 1
Papa's News

"Pass me that knife, please."

Ten-year-old Anna Allerton wiped her hands on the white apron that covered her blue-and-white-checked dress and pushed her blond hair away from her blue eyes. Then she arranged six carrots on the thick butcher block next to the sink. Potatoes, onions, and shelled peas were already lined up along the counter.

Richard, her twelve-year-old brother, handed her the knife. "What are you making?"

"Stew." Chunks of beef simmered in a big black pot on the stove. Anna was ready to add the vegetables. She checked the flame on the new gas stove.

"Do you have to put in onions?" Richard asked, making a sour face.

"Papa likes onions. You can pick them out."

"You sound just like Mama."

Richard lifted the lid on the pot and bent his dark head over it to inspect the meat. Richard took after their French grandmother. His hair and eyes were as dark as Anna's were fair.

"Why don't you stir that, as long as you have the lid off?" Anna handed her brother a spoon.

"Do you think Papa will be home on time?" Richard said. "I don't like burned stew."

"He hasn't telephoned," Anna answered. "He tries to call if he knows he has to stay late at the hospital."

Richard slumped into a chair at the kitchen table. "When your father is a doctor, you have to get used to unpredictable hours."

"That's what Mama always says." Anna attacked the carrots and whacked them into bite-size pieces. "But Uncle Enoch is a banker, and he works long hours, too," she added, using the title her parents insisted the children use as a sign of respect toward their older cousins.

"Downtown Minneapolis is a busy place to do business."

"Uncle Enoch says it's busier every year. He can hardly believe it's 1889 already."

"And Uncle Charles works for the railroad," Richard added. "And his shifts change all the time." He glanced at the pot. "Just don't burn the stew."

Anna rolled her eyes.

Mama came through the door from the dining room.

"How are you doing with supper?"

Anna scooped up a handful of carrots and threw them in the pot. "Everything is on schedule. We just need Papa to come home." She added the potatoes to the pot and stirred the mixture vigorously.

"Put the peas in last," Mama said. "They don't take long to cook."

"I remember." Anna added the onions and left the peas on the counter.

"I'm sure Papa will be here soon." Mama opened a cupboard and removed a stack of large bowls. "Richard, can you get the spoons, please?"

Richard stood up and crossed the kitchen. Just as he pulled open a drawer, they heard the front door open.

"There's Papa," Anna said. She wiped her hands on her apron again and went to greet her father.

"Right on time," Mama said.

Mama and Richard followed Anna to the front door. Eight-year-old Esther was already there, with her arms around her father's neck. He scooped up his youngest child and turned to greet his family.

"Something smells wonderful," Papa said.

"Anna's making stew," Mama informed him.

Papa looked at Anna. "You're becoming quite a cook, young lady."

"I made baking powder biscuits, too," Anna said proudly.

"I can see that." Papa reached out and wiped a smudge of flour from Anna's cheek.

"Will you sit next to me at supper, Papa?" Esther asked.

Papa smiled. "Don't I always?"

"I was just making sure."

"We weren't certain that you would be home on time tonight," Mama said.

Papa put Esther down and sighed. "I wasn't either. The streetcar drivers are threatening to strike."

"A strike?"

"Why?"

"What's a strike?"

"How would we get downtown?"

"One question at a time," Papa said, holding up one hand.

"I'll tell you everything I know."

Anna glanced back toward the kitchen and sat on the edge of a chair.

"You already know," Papa said, "that the streetcar drivers have formed a union. They think that if they bind themselves together as one voice, then they will have more power. They want a raise in their wages."

"They haven't had a raise in a long time," Mama said. "Your cousin Charles reminds us of that all the time."

"But Thomas Lowry, the owner of the Minneapolis Street Railway, says the company is losing money," Papa said. "He can't even afford to pay them the wage they earn now."

Anna pressed her eyebrows together. "Do you think that's true?"

Papa shrugged his shoulders. "I don't know. Some people think he is planning to electrify the streetcars, and that will cost a lot of money."

"Electric streetcars?" Richard said excitedly. "No horses?"

Papa nodded. "It will happen before much longer, I'm sure." He sat down on a sofa.

"I remember when we all went downtown to see the first electric lights on Washington Avenue," Richard said.

Mama chuckled. "You were only five years old. Cousin Abe was sure he had explained everything so that you could understand."

"So if Thomas Lowry pays a higher wage now," Richard said, thinking aloud, "then Mr. Lowry will not be able to afford to electrify the streetcar system."

Papa nodded. "I think that's right."

"Electric streetcars will be good for Minneapolis," Anna said.

"But what about the drivers?" Richard protested. "Is it fair to make their families suffer so we can ride electric cars?"

"What's a strike?" Esther asked, snuggling next to her father on the sofa.

Papa looked down at Esther. "A strike would mean that the drivers would tell Mr. Lowry that they won't drive the streetcars."

"Would they get paid if they did that?"

Papa shook his head. "No, if they don't work, they don't get paid."

Esther was puzzled. "Then they won't get any money. Isn't that worse than not getting a raise?"

Papa laughed. "Now you sound like Uncle Enoch."

"I do?"

"Yes, he says that Mr. Lowry is just making a good business decision. He doesn't force anyone to work for his company. If they don't like the wages, they can look for jobs somewhere else."

"They could work at the flour mills," Anna suggested.

"A lot of people want to work at the mills," Richard said. "It would be hard to get a job there."

"That's exactly what Mr. Lowry thinks," Papa said. "He believes the drivers need their jobs. Not many of them can afford to go without being paid, and he says they won't find better jobs somewhere else."

"Even if they get other jobs," Mama said, "they might have the same problems."

"You're right," Papa added. "Already there have been two hundred strikes in Minnesota in the last ten years."

"But a streetcar strike will hurt a lot of people besides Mr. Lowry," Richard said. "That doesn't seem fair."

Esther sat up straight and sniffed the air. "What's that smell?"

"My stew!" Anna leaped up and flew to the kitchen. She snatched a spoon off the counter and stirred the contents of the pot quickly. The stew was just beginning to stick to the bottom of the pot. But it was not ruined. Thanks to Esther's sensitive nose, supper was saved. Anna sighed in relief. She would have to concentrate better than this, or Mama would not let her cook anymore. She stuck a fork in a potato and decided that the vegetables were tender. The peas, which she added now, would take only a few minutes to cook. It was time to bake the biscuits. Anna was just putting the pan of biscuits in the oven when the rest of her family trailed into the kitchen.

"I told you I don't like burned stew," Richard said.

"It's not burned," Anna assured him.

"You're not going to burn the biscuits, too, are you?" Richard asked.

Anna made a face at him. But she glanced at the oven. She had never made biscuits all by herself before. She wanted them to be perfect.

"Can I have butter on my biscuits?" Esther asked.

"Of course," Mama said. "Why don't you get the butter out and put it on the table."

Mama had left the stack of bowls on the table. She resumed getting the table ready for the meal.

"Richard, we still need spoons for the stew," Mama said.

Papa sat down in his usual chair.

"I had lunch with Charles today," he remarked.

"How are the Fisks?" Mama asked brightly.

"They are doing well. Judith is applying for a job at the Boston Clothing Store on Washington Avenue."

Mama chuckled. "She has loved that store from the time she was two. She would do a wonderful job working there."

"That's what Charles thinks. Teddy is having a hard time settling down in school. His teacher has been sending notes home quite frequently."

Mama smiled. "Well, he is only seven years old. Even Esther

still has a hard time sitting still all day."

"The Fisks are fine," Papa said. "But all this business about the streetcars is taking its toll."

"What do you mean?" Richard asked.

Anna checked the biscuits and stirred the stew. All the while, she listened to what her father had to say.

"Charles is barely talking to Uncle Enoch," Papa said.

"But Enoch is his sister's husband," Mama said. "How can he not talk to them?"

"Oh, he'll talk to Tina. I don't think anything can come between Charles and Tina. And of course Abe and Judith are still the best of friends."

"Those two cousins have always been inseparable," Mama said.

Papa frowned. "It's just that Charles finds it difficult to be around Enoch."

"Charles and Enoch have always been able to see past their differences before," Mama said.

Papa shook his head. "This is different. Charles did not even want to hear me say Enoch's name."

"Is Uncle Charles mad at Uncle Enoch?" Esther asked.

"Let's just say they have a difference of opinion," Papa said. "They're having trouble understanding each other."

"What do the streetcars have to do with them?" Anna asked. Carefully, she lifted the pot of stew from the stove and set it on the table.

"Charles thinks that the streetcar drivers have a right to form a union and go on strike," Papa answered Anna. "It's not only the question of high wages. They also complain that the cars are too open to the elements. They have no protection against the rain, the wind, or the cold."

"And what does Uncle Enoch think?" Richard asked.

"Enoch thinks Thomas Lowry is a good businessman and

11

makes decisions that are good for his company. And Enoch thinks Mr. Lowry has a right to do that. If the street railway company can't make enough money, all the drivers will lose their jobs."

"So maybe it's better if the drivers don't get a raise," Anna said. "That's better than no job at all."

"But doesn't Uncle Enoch think the streetcar company should be fair to the drivers?" Richard asked.

"What if he can't be fair to the drivers and stay in business at the same time?" Papa countered.

"There must be another way to save money."

"Electric streetcars will be cheaper—once Mr. Lowry can afford to buy them and put in the electrical lines."

"Uncle Charles and Uncle Enoch don't work for the street-car company," Anna said. "Why would they quarrel over this?"

"I asked myself the same thing," Papa said. "But Charles is part of the railroad union, so he has a lot of sympathy for the streetcar drivers and their union."

"And Enoch is a banker," Mama said, "so he has sympathy for the businesspeople."

Anna nervously took the biscuits out of the oven. Then she sighed in relief. They were a perfect golden brown and had fluffed up nicely.

"Those look absolutely beautiful, Anna!" Mama said. "I should have let you make biscuits a long time ago."

"I'll put them in a basket," Anna said, her pride showing in her blue eyes.

Mama put a ladle in the pot of stew on the table, and the family took their seats. Bowing her head, Anna listened as her father thanked God for the food. Silently, she added her own prayer: *Please, God, help Uncle Charles and Uncle Enoch to be friends again.*

CHAPTER 2
Who's Right?

"Are you playing baseball today?" Anna asked Richard the next morning.

"Yep. As soon as I'm done here." Richard pulled the broom across the linoleum kitchen floor as rapidly as he could.

"What else does Mama want you to do?" Anna was folding laundry on the kitchen table. She had just brought it in from the clothesline in the backyard.

"Nothing. This is my last chore for the day."

"Is it a practice or a game?" Anna asked, smoothing out one of her cotton skirts.

"Practice. We're getting ready for a game against the Seventh Street team next week." Richard parked the broom in the corner of the kitchen.

"I hope you hit a home run."

"Thanks. I'll be glad just to get a hit."

With his bat propped on his shoulder a few minutes later, Richard started out for the field where he played baseball on Saturday mornings. He had played on the same team for three years. He liked knowing that when he snapped the ball from second base to first, Jack Hammond would be there to tag the base and put the runner out. And when he chased a fly ball into center field, Zachary Davis would move back from the pitcher's mound to cover second base. Zachary was the team's best hurler. Several of the players were very strong hitters, but they were counting on Zach's hurling to beat the Seventh Street Spades.

When they had started playing together, Richard and his friends had been a ragged bunch of bumbling nine year olds. Now they were really a team—the Spitfires. They had given themselves that name because they never ran out of energy. They could depend on each other when they faced a crisis during a game. Richard liked this team, and he hoped they would play together for a long time.

He came to the familiar field.

"Hi, Jack! Hi, Zach!" Richard called across the field.

They ignored him. They were talking to each other, and their faces were getting redder by the second. Richard broke into a trot. When he got closer, he could hear what they were saying.

"If you don't know what you're talking about, then you shouldn't say anything," Jack said.

"Who says I don't know what I'm talking about?" Zach retorted.

"If you knew what you were talking about, you wouldn't say the things you are saying."

"Haven't you heard of free speech? I can say whatever I want to." Zach tossed a ball high in the air and grabbed it forcefully when it came back down.

Richard looked around. Several other boys were watching

Jack and Zach. Tony Tubiera and Tommy Landers scrunched up their faces as they squinted into the early spring sun. Elton Thornton's eyes were wide with excitement about what might happen next. No one seemed to be playing baseball.

"Aren't we going to practice?" Richard asked.

"Yeah, sure," Jack muttered. But he did not move. Neither did Zach.

"So let's get going."

"You go ahead," Zach said.

"We can't practice without you two."

Jack and Zachary stared at each other. No one said anything. Tommy moved his hand to shade his eyes. No one else moved a muscle. Finally Richard could stand it no longer.

"What's the matter?" Richard said. He leaned on his bat.

"Aw, nothing," Jack snarled. "Just go play ball."

"It's not nothing," Zach insisted.

"Then what is it?" Richard asked again.

"Jack's father works for the streetcar company," Zach said.

"I know," Richard answered. "I've ridden in his car lots of times."

"The union is going to ask for a raise," Jack said. "My father deserves a better wage. He works hard."

"I know he works hard," Richard said. "Sometimes it's cold and wet in those cars. And the drivers spend all day out in the weather, no matter how bad it is."

"And he works long hours. He's never home for supper. We hardly see him before we go to bed at night."

"I still don't understand what you two are arguing about," Richard said.

Jack spoke up quickly. "Zach doesn't want to admit that people like my father deserve to be paid for their work."

"He gets paid," Zach muttered.

"Yeah, he gets paid." Tommy Landers had joined the discussion. "If he doesn't like his wage, he can find a new job."

15

"That's right," Elton agreed.

"My father says that the streetcar drivers formed a union so they could bully the owners of the company," Tommy said.

"That's not true!" Tony Tubiera jumped into the discussion. He moved to stand beside Jack Hammond. "Unions protect the workers. My father is in the railroad union."

"So what?" challenged Tommy Landers.

"So he understands unions. When people stand together, they can do more than when they are alone."

"That's a good point," Richard said. "It's like our team. We all need each other, or we will never be able to beat that Seventh Street team. Let's play ball."

Still no one moved. All eyes were on Jack and Zachary. They stood toe to toe, nose to nose. Neither one of them showed any sign of moving.

Richard took a mental inventory of the boys on the team. Tony's father worked for the railroad with Uncle Charles. Jack's father was a streetcar driver. Tommy Landers's parents owned their own shop on Bridge Square, the main business district in Minneapolis. Zach's father worked at the bank where Uncle Enoch worked. Three of the boys had fathers who were managers at the Pillsbury Mills. All the other boys had parents who owned their own small businesses. Only Tony and Jack's fathers were involved with unions.

The team members hardly ever talked about what their parents did for a living. Somehow it had never mattered before. They had been in school together since the first grade. They all lived within a few blocks of each other. Why should they worry about how their parents made a living? They had all ridden in the streetcar that Jack Hammond's father drove. When they did, they enjoyed calling the driver by name. They were riding with a friend. Why should that change, Richard wondered, just because of a union?

Richard always looked forward to Saturday mornings—but

not because he wanted to listen to a dispute about unions. He wanted to play baseball.

"Let's do what we came here to do," Richard said. He snapped his bat through the air in anticipation.

But Jack was not ready. "Unions are not a game," Jack said. "And Thomas Lowry, the owner of the streetcar company, is not interested in team spirit. He just wants to make money."

"He has to run a good business," Zach said, "or the whole company will go broke."

"He doesn't have to make himself filthy rich at the expense of all the drivers."

"Is that what your father says?"

"Yeah."

"He's just jealous of Thomas Lowry."

"That's the nuttiest idea I've ever heard."

Richard stepped back from the group and practiced swinging his bat, but with less enthusiasm than before. At first, Jack and Zachary were both making good points. But now they were sniping at each other. And why did they have to discuss this now, on the baseball field? Richard whipped the bat through the air and imagined that he had hit the ball so hard that it would sail into the next block. He really wanted to play baseball.

"Come on," Richard pleaded. "Let's practice. If we don't, that Seventh Street team will wipe the floor with us."

"I'm not worried about them," Zach said. "They're just a bunch of union sympathizers. Most of their fathers work for the railroad."

"What does that have to do with how well they play ball?" Jack challenged. "Are you saying you're a better baseball player because your father works in a bank?"

"I didn't say that," Zachary said in his own defense.

Richard sighed. "Come on, Zach. You've seen the Seventh Street team play before. You know they'll be tough to beat."

"Yeah, I know," Zach muttered.

"So can we practice now?"

"Let's get started."

"Good. Why don't you hurl, and we'll have batting practice."

"Okay."

The team took their places. Zachary stood on the pitcher's mound. Richard stationed himself behind the plate to be the catcher. Three others took places in the field to retrieve the balls that would be hit. The rest of the team lined up to take their turns at batting practice.

Tommy Landers swung and missed four balls in a row. Finally, he hit one, but it only dribbled toward third base. He would have been out in a real game. Richard groaned inwardly. They would have to do better than that against the Spades.

Tony Tubiera was next. He smacked the first pitch out to center field and trotted around the bases triumphantly. He was already back to home plate before the fielders could find the ball and throw it back in.

"That's the way to do it!" Richard said, as he clapped Tony on the back. "We're going to need a lot of long balls to beat that team. We can count on you!"

Jack Hammond stepped up to the plate next. Zachary stared at him for a long time before throwing the first ball. Jack let it pass. From the catcher's position, Richard thought it was a good pitch. He lobbed the ball back to Zach.

Jack had barely moved. Now he dug his feet more solidly into the ground.

The second pitch to Jack was too high. Richard had to jump to keep it from going over his head and landing behind him. He tossed it back to Zach again.

"Come on, Jack," Tommy Landers called from the infield. "This is batting practice, not looking practice."

Jack paid no attention to Tommy. He squared himself once again to meet Zach's pitch. Zach wound up and let the pitch fly.

From the instant Zach released the ball, Richard knew it was a bad pitch. It was zooming in too close to Jack's head—far too close. Jack stumbled backward, trying not to lose his balance.

For a moment, Richard was sure that Jack was going to charge at Zachary. No doubt Zach would say that he had not meant to throw the ball at Jack's head. But Jack would never believe that. Even Richard had to agree that Zach was too good a pitcher to lose control. And now he had thrown two high pitches in a row.

Before throwing the ball back to Jack, Richard hesitated. He casually stepped between Jack and Zachary, then glanced at Jack. Jack's wide jaw was set. He was angry. But his feet had not moved. Richard tossed the ball to Zach and took his place behind home plate. Jack's knuckles tightened around his bat until they turned white. But he stayed where he was.

Zach leaned forward with his hands on his knees and glared at Jack. It was as if he were daring Jack to react. Jack stayed put. He licked his lips and kept his focus, waiting for the next pitch.

Finally, Zachary wound up and let the ball fly. The pitch was a little high and a little outside the strike zone. But Jack was ready to prove his worth to the team. He smacked that ball farther than anyone on the team had ever hit a ball before. The players in the outfield scrambled to find the ball in the tall grass beyond their playing field.

Jack started running, then slowed almost to a walk. It would be a long time before they found the ball. As he rounded second base, he fixed his gaze on Zachary again.

Zach was sitting on the pitcher's mound, shaking his head.

Richard had come to the field to play ball. So he ignored the glaring war between Zachary and Jack. Instead he whooped and cheered Jack on. "All you have to do is hit like that against the Spades, and we'll have no problem!"

Jack broke his lock on Zach's face and grinned at Richard.

CHAPTER 3

A Friendship Ends

Monday morning came too soon. All day Sunday, Richard wondered about Jack and Zachary. How long could they stay mad at each other? Neither of them could change what was happening in the streetcar company. But they could play baseball together, just as they had for three years. Richard had dreaded Monday morning, when he would have to go to school and see Zachary and Jack.

Mama believed in observing the Sabbath. After church on Sunday, she liked the family to spend the afternoon together in quiet activities. Richard usually read a book. He was in the middle of *Twenty Thousand Leagues under the Sea,* a Jules Verne novel. His cousin Abe Stevenson had recommended the book to him. But even the fantastic imagination of a science fiction writer like Jules Verne could not distract Richard. All day Sunday he wondered how Jack and Zachary could go from being best friends to hated enemies. Hadn't they ever really liked each other—the way Richard liked both of them?

Now Monday morning had come. Richard and Anna entered the schoolyard. Anna was a few steps ahead of Richard, which was unusual. She had a very small build and short legs. She nearly always had trouble keeping up with Richard's long stride. With her book bag over one shoulder, she turned to look at her brother.

"Don't you feel well, Richard?" she asked.

"I feel fine," he muttered.

"You look fine, too," Anna observed. "But you're not acting fine. What's the matter?"

"Nothing."

"I don't believe that for a minute. You've been acting strangely ever since Saturday."

"What do you mean?"

"For one thing, you sat still all the way through church yesterday, even when we sang that hymn that you think has such a funny tune."

Richard shrugged. "So what?"

"So, I think something's wrong. Something happened at your baseball practice. That's when it started."

Richard gave in. He knew Anna would keep after him until he told her what was wrong.

"Zachary and Jack had a fight at the practice," Richard said. "It's about the unions. They were so mad at each other that they didn't want to play. Zach threw a ball that almost hit Jack's head."

"On purpose?"

"It was hard to tell."

Anna glanced across the schoolyard. "Here comes Jack now.

Zach is right behind him, but they're not talking to each other."

"See what I mean? They've been best friends since they were little, and now they don't want to talk to each other."

"It doesn't make sense." Anna shifted her attention to another corner of the schoolyard. "Who is that new girl over there?"

Richard followed her gaze to a girl Anna's age who sat timidly on a bench alone. "Oh, that's Kjersten Olsson. Her family just came from Sweden."

"How do you know them?" Anna asked.

"Uncle Charles told me about them. Mr. Olsson was looking for a job with the railroad. Charles wanted to hire him, but he doesn't have any openings right now."

"So did Mr. Olsson find another job?"

Richard shook his head. "I don't think so. But Charles says that Mr. Olsson wants Kjersten to start right out getting an education. He made sure she would start school right away."

"I'll have to be sure to talk to her."

"Good luck," Richard said, chuckling. "She doesn't speak English."

"Not any?"

"No. They just arrived from Sweden last week."

"She's probably lonely, then. There aren't any other Swedish children in our school."

"Most of them don't live around here. But the Olssons are renting a house in the neighborhood until they find someplace to settle down."

A door on the front of the school opened, and a teacher came out. She pulled vigorously on the rope that moved the brass bell atop the building. The bell clanked, instantly commanding the attention of every student in the schoolyard.

Anna laughed. "There's your teacher. Miss Wickham means business today."

Richard groaned. "Probably she'll give us a math quiz."

"I'm glad I'm not in your class."

"Just wait until next year."

Inside the school door, Richard and Anna separated. There were four different classes in the small building, covering eight grades. Richard walked down the hall to his classroom. Standing at the back of the classroom, he wished he could choose a new seat. Miss Wickham had assigned him a seat behind Jack and across the aisle from Zachary. When the assignments were made, all three boys were ecstatic. Now, Richard knew, Zach and Jack would feel differently. Reluctantly, Richard took his seat. Jack came in and sat in front of him.

"Hi, Richard."

"Hi, Jack."

Zach was already sitting across the aisle. Jack did not say a word to him. But Richard could not ignore Zach.

"Good morning, Zach," he said.

"Morning," Zachary muttered without looking up from his desk.

Miss Wickham had threatened to give a math quiz, but she didn't. Richard was relieved. He was not sure he would be able to concentrate well enough to take a test, and he dreaded the thought of what might happen between Zach and Jack during lunch.

Anna spotted the new girl at the other side of her classroom, but there was no way to talk with her. Finally lunchtime came. The students burst out the doors of the school with their lunch buckets and scattered around the schoolyard to enjoy the April spring day.

Anna was one of the last ones out of the building. She looked around. She wanted to talk to Kjersten—or at least try to. At last she spotted the fair-headed girl sitting on a bench on the far side of the schoolyard. She was unpacking her meager lunch.

Anna approached her. "Hello," she said brightly.

Kjersten looked up, confused. Finally, she forced a smile.

"I know you don't speak English," Anna said, "but I want to be your friend."

Kjersten wrinkled her forehead in concentration. Anna knew she had not understood anything.

"You have to learn English," Anna said, "or you won't be able to learn anything else at school."

"English?" Kjersten said, finally recognizing a word.

"Yes, English. You must learn." Anna sat down on the bench next to Kjersten. "When my little sister was learning to talk, my mother said that the most important thing was that we all talk to her a lot. So that's what I'm going to do with you. I'm just going to talk until you understand."

Anna smiled at Kjersten, who smiled back blankly.

"I can't imagine what it must be like not to understand anything around you," Anna said, as she unwrapped her sandwich. "But it can't be very pleasant. You're going to have to learn very quickly, because you don't want to be miserable forever."

Anna peeled her sandwich apart and held up a slice of Mama's fresh bread. "Bread," she said slowly and distinctly. "Bread."

Kjersten looked at the lunch in her lap. She had fruit and a sausage.

"No, you don't have any bread," Anna said. "But you know what bread is. Just say the word." And she dangled the bread in front of Kjersten once more.

"Brud?" Kjersten said timidly.

Anna was very careful not to laugh. "Almost. Try again. Bread." She spoke as distinctly as she could.

"Bruad," Kjersten croaked.

"That's better," Anna said. "You just have to practice. Bread."

"Bruad. Bruad. Brrread."

"There you go!" Now Anna pointed at the fruit in Kjersten's lap. "Apple."

Kjersten picked up the sausage and said, "Uppa."

"No, that one," Anna said, pointing again. This time she had her finger nearly on the fruit. "Apple."

Kjersten picked up the apple. "Appo?"

"Apple."

Anna repeated the word as many times as Kjersten needed to hear it before she could say it correctly.

"Eat," Anna said, and she took a bite of her bread.

"Eat," Kjersten echoed perfectly.

"That's an easy word, isn't it?" Anna said. "There are lots of easy words. Maybe we should learn those first."

Kjersten smiled and bit her apple. Anna thought it was a true smile.

In between bites of her own lunch, Anna continued talking.

"Is our teacher helping you at all?" she asked. "I suppose Miss Marks knows that you don't speak English. But she has so many other students that she won't have time to teach you any words. That's all right, because I can do it. I'll have to find out where you live, though. We won't see each other enough at school."

Kjersten smiled again. Anna could see the anxiety in her blue eyes.

"You have no idea what I'm saying," Anna said, "but I hope you know that I'm trying to be your friend." She reached out and touched Kjersten's blond braid hanging over one shoulder. "I've always wondered what I might look like with braided hair. My mother says that I have such beautiful hair that I shouldn't tie it up in knots. But I think you look very pretty."

Anna twisted the ends of her own hair between her fingers.

She and Kjersten both had blond hair and blue eyes.

"Hair," Anna said.

"Eeaare," Kjersten croaked.

"Hair." Again Anna repeated the word as many times as Kjersten needed. She glanced across the schoolyard at Richard. "I wonder if you have any brothers."

Richard had settled under a tree by himself with his lunch. Concentrating on their schoolwork, Zachary and Jack had not had much time during the morning to pay any attention to each other. But Richard had still felt trapped between them. Now he could see Jack coming toward him. Richard glanced around. Zachary was off to one side, gently tossing a baseball between his hands.

"Hi, Richard," Jack said. "Are you finished eating?"

"Almost."

"We still have a few minutes before the bell rings. How about playing catch?"

Richard hesitated. Out of the corner of his eye, he saw Zachary looking in his direction. What would Zachary think if he tossed a ball with Jack?

"I think I need to let my lunch settle," Richard finally said.

"Come on, Richard, just a few throws?"

"Maybe later." Richard stuffed a piece of cheese in his mouth and tried to look busy eating.

Jack shuffled off. But as soon as he was gone, Zachary made a beeline for Richard.

"What did Jack want?" Zach demanded.

"He just wanted to play catch," Richard answered.

"But you didn't want to play with him, did you?"

Richard shrugged. "I said I wasn't finished eating."

Zach bent over and looked in Richard's lunch bucket. "It looks like you're finished now. Let's find a bat and hit a few balls."

Richard's stomach sank. He'd been afraid Zach was going to ask that question.

"Like I told Jack," Richard said, "I want to let my lunch settle."

"You never wanted your lunch to settle before," countered Zach. "You don't even like to eat lunch."

"Well today I ate lunch, and I want it to settle."

"You're ignoring me, just like Jack. Are you on his side?"

"I'm not on anybody's side," Richard said. "I just want to eat my lunch."

Across the schoolyard, Anna saw the frustration rising in her brother's face. She imagined what Jack and Zachary must have said to Richard. She could see his tension in the way he held his head. Jack and Zachary and Richard had been friends for a long time—long before they formed a baseball team together. They used to be just little boys who played together. When did it start to matter whether their fathers were in unions or not? Anna wondered.

"Don't worry," she said aloud to Kjersten. "We'll be friends because we want to be. None of this other business will matter."

Kjersten nodded seriously as if she understood. Knowing she did not, Anna smiled in amusement.

CHAPTER 4

On Strike

"Why didn't you call me when you were ready to start cooking?" Anna lifted the lid on one pot to see what Mama was fixing. "I would have come to help you."

"You were doing homework," Mama answered. "I don't like to interrupt you when you're studying."

"I would rather cook."

"Studying is important. You can slice some cheese to have with the soup."

Anna opened the icebox and removed a chunk of cheddar cheese. Picking up a knife, she asked, "Mama, do you know any Swedish words?"

"Swedish?" Mama was puzzled.

"Don't you have any Swedish friends?"

"Well, yes, I know a couple of Swedish women at church, but they've been in Minneapolis for several years. They speak English."

"Don't you ever hear them speaking Swedish to each other?"

"Sometimes they do. I never paid much attention to what they were saying. Why are you suddenly so interested in Swedish?"

"There's a new girl at school. She's in my class, and she doesn't speak any English."

Mama smiled. "Are you going to try to teach her English?"

Anna nodded. "She seems like a very nice girl. I sit with her at lunch some days. But I wish I knew a few words that she could understand."

"Why don't you ask her?"

"What do you mean?"

"When you teach her the English word for something, find out the Swedish word."

Anna thought about her mother's suggestion. "I should have thought of that. I've been too busy teaching her to pronounce 'sandwich.' "

Richard appeared at the back door off the kitchen.

"Oh, good," he said, pulling the door open and dropping his book bag to the floor. "You haven't served supper yet. I was afraid I was late."

Mama glanced at the clock. "As a matter of fact, you are late—very late. But so is your father. I've been waiting for him." She picked up a wooden spoon and stirred the bean soup.

"Is it sticking to the bottom?" Anna asked.

"It's starting to. If he doesn't come home soon, we'll have to start without him."

"Oh, no, let's wait," Anna pleaded. "I like it when we all eat together."

"I don't want to eat burned food," Richard said.

"You won't." Anna stirred the soup some more.

Esther came in from the dining room. "I'm hungry," she grumbled. "When will supper be ready?"

"It's ready now," Richard said.

"Good." Esther climbed into a chair. "Let's eat."

"We're waiting for Papa," Anna said.

"Do we have to?" Esther whined. "I'm sooo hungry."

Mama glanced at the clock again. "I don't understand why he didn't telephone if he was going to be this late."

"That is strange," Richard agreed.

"There must have been an emergency," Anna suggested.

"Yes, I suppose so," Mama murmured.

For another ten minutes, they stirred the pot of soup and speculated about why Papa was so late.

"I'm starving to death!" Esther declared dramatically. "We can save some food for Papa. Please, let's eat."

Mama sighed and glanced at the clock once more.

"I suppose we might as well," she said. She reached for a stack of bowls and started dishing up the soup.

Esther carried hers to the table and picked up her spoon.

"Wait until we give thanks," Mama said.

Esther sighed and put down her spoon.

A few minutes later, Mama, Anna, Richard, and Esther sat before their steaming bowls of navy bean soup with bread and meat and cheese on the platter in the middle of the table. Mama gave thanks to God for the food. Anna prayed silently that Papa would be safe.

"Finally!" Esther said, as she plunged her spoon into her soup and slurped up the first mouthful.

Just then the back door opened.

"Papa!" Anna cried.

"Daniel, are you all right?" Mama asked. She rose to her feet to greet him.

Papa kissed Mama's cheek. "I'm sorry I didn't call," he said. "By the time I realized I should call, I wasn't anywhere near a phone."

"You look exhausted," Anna said.

"What happened, Papa?" Richard asked.

Papa took off his coat and hung it over the back of a kitchen chair.

"Just let me get settled and I'll tell you all the whole story," Papa said.

Mama dished up Papa's soup and they all sat down again.

Papa took a bite of bread and then began his story.

"I was so busy today that I hardly noticed what was going on downtown," he said. "I saw nearly two dozen patients at the clinic this morning. Then, after lunch, I went over to the hospital to make my rounds. I thought it was odd that there were no streetcars around. But I didn't have far to go, so I paid no attention.

"Later, another doctor told me that Thomas Lowry had announced a cut in the wages of the streetcar drivers—two cents an hour!"

"But the drivers already make so little money," Richard said. He thought of Jack Hammond and wondered how his friend would take the news.

Papa nodded. "I know. I knew Mr. Lowry would not want to give the drivers the raise they wanted. But I did not think he would cut their wages even lower."

"What will the drivers do now?" Anna asked. She passed the platter of meat and cheese to her father.

"They won't drive the streetcars, that's for sure," Papa said. "They went on strike." He took a bite of the cheese Anna had sliced.

"Strike?" Esther asked.

"Yes, a strike. The drivers refuse to drive until Mr. Lowry gives back their wages."

"So that's why there were no streetcars when you went out," Mama said.

Papa nodded. "As word spread around the city, the drivers turned back to the car barns. They stabled the horses and hung up their reins. By the middle of the afternoon, no streetcars were running anywhere in the city."

"None at all?" Richard asked.

Papa shook his head. "None."

"But there are over two hundred streetcars."

"Not today. Not even one."

"It's hard to imagine Minneapolis without streetcars," Anna said.

"We'll all have to get used to it," Papa said. "I don't think this will be settled easily." He chewed on his cheese. "Of course, I didn't realize when I left the hospital that the street-cars weren't running. When I set out for home, I thought I would pick one up along the way. As I said, by the time I realized there were no streetcars, I was far from a telephone. I had no choice but to walk the rest of the way home."

"It's a long way," Mama said. "No wonder it took you so long."

"At least I wasn't alone." He folded a piece of bread around a chunk of cheese. "Everyone who works downtown was in the same situation. We all had to walk."

"What about Uncle Enoch?" Anna asked. "He has a lame leg. It's hard for him to walk that far."

"I thought of him," Papa said.

"Did you see him leaving the bank?"

"No, I didn't see him. And there was nothing I could do for him anyway. We don't own a carriage."

"No," Mama said. "We've always depended on the street-cars."

"Uncle Enoch doesn't have a carriage, either," Anna said.

"How will he get to work every day without the streetcars?"

Papa shrugged. "I'm not sure what Enoch will do. But I know he thinks Mr. Lowry did the right thing."

"Perhaps we should think about getting a carriage and a horse of our own," Mama said.

"Surely the strike will be settled soon," Richard said.

Papa shook his head again. "I wouldn't count on that. As I walked home, I listened to what people were saying in the streets. Mr. Lowry is a very stubborn man. No one believes he will negotiate with the drivers. Either they do things his way or they don't work."

"But that's not fair," Richard said. "He should at least talk to the drivers. Maybe if they understood each other better, they would figure something out that would make both sides happy."

"That's not likely."

Anna and Richard had stopped eating. Only Esther continued to happily slurp her way through the meal.

"What will happen now?" Richard asked. Images of Jack and Zachary standing toe to toe filled his mind.

Papa sighed. "I'm not sure. I don't think anyone can say. Mr. Lowry might hire other men to drive the streetcars."

"Can he do that?"

"Yes, he can. It's his company. He doesn't have to do what the union tells him to do."

"That doesn't seem fair to the drivers," Richard said.

"Mr. Lowry is not concerned about the drivers. His concern is for his company."

"But the drivers are his company," Anna said emphatically.

"He doesn't see it that way," Papa said. "His income comes from the passengers. He has to keep the cars running, or he won't make any money at all."

"If he gave the drivers their wages back, he wouldn't have

any trouble keeping the cars running," Mama reasoned.

Papa shook his head. "I don't think he will do that."

Richard twirled his spoon in his soup and stared absently at the bread platter.

"Richard, Anna, you must eat," Mama prodded.

"I've lost my appetite," Richard said. He put his spoon down.

"You must eat anyway," Mama said. "I know this strike will upset a lot of people, but that's no reason to starve yourself."

"Papa," Richard said, "did you happen to see Mr. Hammond downtown? You know, Jack's father."

"No, Richard, I'm sorry. I didn't see him. He must have gone home earlier in the day."

"Oh."

"You'll see Jack tomorrow at school, won't you?"

Richard nodded.

"You can ask him how his father is."

Richard did not answer. He could not help thinking about what Zachary would say to Jack. He was not sure he wanted to be around when Jack and Zach met the next day.

"I wonder what Uncle Charles thinks about all this," Anna said. "I know he likes the unions. He belongs to one."

"I'm sure he supports the strike," Papa said. "He knows how businesses can take advantage of employees."

"It's not fair," Richard said.

"No, it's not," his father agreed.

"It's not fair of the company to cut the wages of the drivers. But it's not fair for the drivers to go on strike, either."

"What good will the strike do?" Anna asked. "If Mr. Lowry finds other men to drive the streetcars for less money, how does that help people like the Hammonds?"

"It doesn't," Richard said. "That's why it's not fair. Nobody is helped. Everybody is hurt."

"It sure seems that way to us," Mama said.

"I can't understand why Mr. Hammond would go on strike," Richard said. "He needs his job. And I think he even likes his job. He's always telling stories and joking with the passengers."

"Oh, I know he likes his job," Papa said. "I've heard him say so. But he's a member of the union. If the union votes to go on strike, then all the members go on strike."

"Even if they don't want to?"

"The strength of the union comes from everyone banding together," Papa explained. "If some of the drivers cooperate with Mr. Lowry, then the rest of the drivers will suffer even more. They have to act together, as if they were one person. That's the only way the union can have any power against the company."

Richard nodded. "I know. I've heard Uncle Charles explain about unions. But it still doesn't make sense to me. Even if all the union members join together as one big person, they are still not as powerful as Mr. Lowry. He owns the company."

"Yes, but he cannot operate the company without drivers," Papa said.

"So they need each other," Anna said.

"It just might take awhile before both sides realize how much they need each other."

"I hate to think what this will do to Charles and Enoch's relationship," Mama said. "Alison and Tina will be pulling their hair out trying to find ways to make their husbands get along."

Papa sighed heavily and pushed his empty plate away. "Let's just pray that someone finds a solution to the strike very soon."

CHAPTER 5
The Union Prepares

"Come on, Richard," Anna said urgently. She stood near the front door, ready to go. "Kjersten will be waiting. Let's go."

"Tell me again what we're doing," Richard said. He looked up from the book he was reading in the living room after school.

"I told Kjersten I would take her downtown. She hasn't even seen Bridge Square yet. And I want to show her the shops."

"But it's getting late. The shops will not be open much longer."

"That's all right because we're not really shopping. We're just looking. But Mama says I can't go alone."

"That's right," Mama said, glancing up from the newspaper. "I'm not sure you should go at all."

"Aw, Mama!" Anna grumbled.

"There's an article right here in today's newspaper talking about the strike," Mama said. "A lot of people out on the streets are angry. The police have had to break up several fistfights."

"We'll be careful, Mama," Anna promised. "I already promised Kjersten, and she hasn't got a telephone. I don't want to disappoint her."

"What do you think, Daniel?" Mama said.

Papa put down the business section of the paper and looked at Anna. "I think," he said slowly, "that Anna should have talked to us before she made a promise to Kjersten."

"Please, Papa," Anna pleaded.

"I understand your mother's concerns," Papa said, "and you will have to be extra careful. Can you promise me that?"

"Yes, yes! We'll be sooo careful!"

"Daniel, are you sure about this?" Mama asked doubtfully.

"They're just children," Papa said. "They're not members of any union. I don't think anyone will bother with them."

"But they could get caught in the middle of something."

"That's why we're sending Richard along," Papa said. "Between the two of them, Richard and Anna have enough sense to stay out of trouble."

"So we can go?" Anna said hopefully.

"Yes, you may go," Papa answered.

Anna looked at Mama.

"If you insist on going," Mama said, "at least take a jar of preserves to Mrs. Olsson."

Outside, Richard and Anna walked along for several blocks.

"This is not the way to Bridge Square," Richard said.

"I know. But it's the way to Kjersten's house."

"How far away does she live?"

"About a mile, I think."

"So we have to walk a mile in the wrong direction?"

"It's not the wrong direction. It's the way to Kjersten's house."

"But then we have to walk all the way back again, and then the rest of the way to Bridge Square. And then we have to come all the way back to bring Kjersten home. That's going to be at least four miles."

Anna shrugged. "We have time."

"Under the circumstances, I think Kjersten would understand if you did not show up at her house."

"There's no reason to disappoint her," Anna said with determination. And she walked a little faster.

"If we could ride the streetcar, I wouldn't mind," Richard said.

"Look!" Anna said, pointing. "There's a streetcar. And it's going our direction." She put out her hand to hail the driver.

Richard grabbed Anna's arm and yanked her back from the edge of the street.

"Ow!" Anna protested.

"What do you think you're doing?" Richard hissed.

"You said you wanted to ride a streetcar. And here's a car now. The driver must not be part of the strike."

"All the drivers are on strike," Richard said emphatically. "This driver is a scab."

"A scab?"

"One of the men Thomas Lowry hired to drive the cars in place of the regular drivers. He makes the new drivers promise not to join a union."

The streetcar rattled closer to them. The driver glanced at them hopefully. Richard pulled Anna farther away from the road. The car rumbled on.

"No one was riding in the car," Anna said.

"That's right," Richard said.

"But why is Mr. Lowry paying men to drive empty cars?"

"He hopes people will get tired of walking and start riding."

"But you don't think so, do you?" Anna asked. "Just a few minutes ago, you were wishing you could ride a streetcar, but when you had the chance, you wouldn't get on."

Richard shook his head. "It's not safe. I promised Mama and Papa I would look out for you."

"What would happen if we got on a streetcar?" Anna asked. "If no one else is in the car, how could we get hurt?"

Richard glanced around. "Do you see those people at the next corner?"

Anna nodded. One block away stood a woman and three young men who looked like they had nowhere to go.

"If we get on," Richard said, "they'll get on. They'll call the driver names and lecture us all the way downtown about destroying everything the union has worked for."

Anna looked at her brother. "How do you know all this?"

"I talked to Jack Hammond."

"I thought you were not getting along with Jack."

"I have nothing against Jack," Richard said. "I don't understand why he's fighting with Zachary, but I'm trying to be friends with both of them."

"So what did Jack tell you?"

"His father was thinking about going back to work. Jack's mama is worried they won't have enough money from the sewing she takes in. But Mr. Hammond said it was not worth all the trouble it would stir up." Richard started walking again. "Besides, it doesn't matter now. There won't be another car along this way for a long time."

It took Richard and Anna almost an hour to walk to Kjersten's house and retrace their steps to go to Bridge Square. As they approached the downtown area, Kjersten's blue eyes lit up with a fresh glow. She raced ahead of Richard and Anna, her braids bobbing over her shoulders. Every few steps, Kjersten

39

glanced over her shoulder to make sure Anna was behind her, but she could not make herself slow down.

Knowing that Kjersten could not understand him, Richard said to Anna, "I've never seen someone so excited about seeing a bridge."

"Bridge?" Kjersten said, repeating the word Anna had taught her a few days ago.

"We've always lived in Minneapolis," Anna said. "We've seen the bridges our whole lives. If we visited Sweden, we'd be interested in things that other people think are ordinary."

"I suppose so," Richard muttered.

They were on Hennepin Avenue now, heading for the heart of downtown Minneapolis. In a few minutes they would be at Bridge Square. From there they could look at the huge Pillsbury A mill across the river. Richard hoped there would be trains on the stone arch bridge that carried Jim Hill's railroad across the surging Mississippi River.

Kjersten's blue eyes were bright with excitement. She darted from one shop to another, pointing and questioning with her eyes. Smiling, Anna answered as many questions as she could.

Suddenly Anna stopped and pointed.

"Richard, look! Isn't that Uncle Charles?"

Richard peered down the street. "Yes, and it looks like Abe is with him."

Anna quickened her steps. "Let's go say hello."

As they got closer, they saw that Uncle Charles and his eighteen-year-old nephew, Abe, were not just out for an afternoon stroll. Their hands were full of pamphlets, and they were handing one to every person who passed by.

"What is it?" Anna asked.

"Union literature," Richard answered. He slowed his steps. "Why don't we just go on by? They look busy."

"Don't be silly," Anna said. "We can't pretend that we didn't see them."

"They haven't noticed us yet," Richard countered.

Just then, Abe waved a long arm.

"Now they have," Anna said.

Kjersten looked confused, but she followed where Anna led.

"Hello, Uncle Charles. Hello, Abe," Anna said cheerfully. "I would like you to meet my friend, Kjersten."

"Glad to meet you, Kjersten," Uncle Charles said. "What brings you downtown on this fine afternoon?"

"She doesn't speak English," Richard said.

Abe's eyes widened slightly. "Not at all?"

"Only the words Anna has taught her."

"Oh, I understand," Uncle Charles said. He turned to Anna. "So I'll ask you what has brought you downtown today."

"Kjersten just moved to Minneapolis two weeks ago. I wanted to show her around." She gestured toward the stack of papers under her older cousin's arm. "Why are you here?"

"We have a union meeting beginning in a few minutes," Uncle Charles explained. "We're asking people to come inside and hear a speaker."

"Is it about the strike?" Anna asked.

Uncle Charles nodded. "The strike will not be settled if people cannot learn to listen to one another."

"I suppose that's true."

Richard wondered if Uncle Enoch knew that his son Abraham was passing out union literature. Surely Uncle Enoch would not approve. He was already unhappy that Abe had taken a job with the railroad while he got ready to go to college. But Richard decided not to say anything.

"Are there many people in there?" Anna asked, pointing to a brick building.

"There is still room for more." Uncle Charles reached out

41

and handed a pamphlet to a man passing by.

"We'd better go in soon," Abe said.

"All right," his uncle replied. He handed a pamphlet to Richard. "Here, take this home to your father."

"My father is not a union man," Richard said.

"But he's not against the union, either," Uncle Charles said. "He might be interested in what we have to say."

Uncle Charles and Abe disappeared inside the brick building.

"What does the pamphlet say?" Anna asked.

Richard turned it over and looked at the front. "Stand together," he read. "The strength of many, the mind of one."

"The strength of many, the mind of one," Anna repeated. "I like that."

Richard looked up from the paper and into his sister's blue eyes.

"Are you thinking what I'm thinking?" Anna asked.

Richard nodded slowly. "But just for a few minutes. After all, you promised to show Kjersten the bridge, and soon it will be time to take her home."

Anna nodded. "I just want to see what it's like."

Once again, Kjersten did not understand what was happening, but she followed where Anna led—into the brick building.

Inside, they crept down a dark stairwell and came to a set of double doors.

"It must be in there," Richard whispered, peeking through the crack between the two doors. His jaw dropped. "There must be three hundred people in that room."

"Open the door," Anna urged.

"Are you sure?" Richard asked.

Anna nodded. Kjersten looked from Richard to Anna and back again.

Richard opened the door, and the three of them slipped into the back of the room.

In the front of the room on a makeshift stage, a man stood on a chair.

"The mayor is making promises he can't keep," the man shouted. "He promises to protect the drivers. He threatens to arrest anyone who gets in the way of the smooth operation of the streetcar system."

The crowd booed and rumbled.

"This city does not have enough police officers for the mayor to keep that promise," the man shouted, thrusting his fist in the air. "We have people standing on every corner watching the cars. We know who is riding and who is not."

"See?" Richard whispered. "Isn't that what I told you?"

"Shhh!" Anna said.

The man on the chair continued. "This is not the first strike in Minneapolis, and it will not be the last. Organized labor will grow in strength, grow in numbers, grow in influence."

The crowd cheered. Richard spotted Uncle Charles in one corner. He was starting to applaud.

"The day of management's power is past," the man said. "We are entering a more humane era. In the future, a man who gives an honest day's work will get an honest day's wage. He will use that wage to care for his family, to bring up his children in dignity."

The crowd roared and chanted, "Stand together, stand together."

Kjersten clutched Anna's arm so tightly it hurt. "What mean?" she said. Her blue eyes had lost their glow and become frightened.

Anna sighed and said quietly, "If only I could explain it to you. Your father would understand. It's the same reason he brought you here—the reason he wants you to go to a good school."

Kjersten searched Anna's face with questioning eyes.

"We'd better go," Richard said.

CHAPTER 6

Kjersten's Problem

"We sit here?" Kjersten asked hopefully.

"Very good!" Anna exclaimed. "Yes, we'll sit here. With a cotton handkerchief, she dusted off a wooden bench. "Now, I know you've never seen a baseball game before, so I'll try to explain the rules."

Kjersten peered at the baseball diamond, with the shapeless white sandbags evenly spaced.

"One team will try to hit the ball and run all the way around," Anna explained. "They have to touch all the bases. The other team will try to stop them. Each team gets three outs, and there are nine innings."

Kjersten looked at Anna, completely confused.

"I never realized how complicated it is to explain baseball," Anna said. "You'll get the idea when they start playing a real game."

Richard had talked for weeks about playing the team from Seventh Street. Apparently many of the other players had, too. Quite a few family members had turned out to watch the match. Anna was surprised to see some of her friends from school. Some of the girls had brothers on Richard's team.

Anna turned and waved to a row of girls behind her. No one waved back. Instead, Anna saw several of them put their heads together. She could tell from the way their shoulders were moving that they were laughing. Samantha Landers glanced up at Anna. But instead of catching Anna's eyes, she quickly turned her head back to the huddle.

"Baseball," Kjersten said very distinctly. She gestured as if she were throwing a ball.

"Very good," Anna said. She gestured as if she were swinging a bat and said, "Bat."

"Bat. Bat." Kjersten echoed.

Behind them, Anna heard another echo. She twisted around to see her friend Martha Wilkerson saying, "Baht, baht. Ja, ja, dis ist baht."

Alice and Samantha burst into giggles. "Ja, ja."

Anna stared at Martha. Martha stared back.

"Martha Wilkerson, you stop that!" Anna demanded.

Alice and Samantha giggled even harder.

Anna turned to face the field again, her arms crossed on her chest. "Never mind them," she said to Kjersten. "We have a ball game to watch."

Both teams were finishing their warm-ups. Soon it would be time to begin playing. Richard did not seem to be concentrating on the warm-up, however. His eyes were raised to the outfield. Zachary had not shown up for the game. Richard kept hoping that Zach was just late. But as the minutes dragged by, he was forced to admit that Zach was not coming. He might never come to play on their team again. Zach was their best hurler. Without him throwing the ball, the team could be in for a great deal of trouble on the field.

"He's not coming, is he?" Tommy Landers said to Richard. Richard shook his head. "I guess not."

"Maybe he's sick," Tommy said.

"Naw," said another boy, "I saw him on Bridge Square this morning. He's fine."

"Maybe his parents wouldn't let him play today," Richard speculated. "Maybe they had relatives visiting or something."

"Naw, they come to all the games. More likely they wouldn't let him play because they don't want him on this team anymore."

"That's ridiculous," Richard said. "He's played on this team for three years. They never minded before."

"It's different now."

"No, it's not. It's the same team."

"Now Jack's father and Zach's father are on opposite sides of the strike."

"So what?" Richard said. "That doesn't mean they can't play baseball together."

"Yes, it does." It was Tony Tubiera's turn to speak. "My parents didn't want me to come, either. Most of you are management families."

"We're just families!" Richard insisted. "And we're the same team we've always been."

"Yeah, well today we're playing without Zachary on the mound," Tommy said. "I have a feeling we'd better get used to it."

Jack Hammond had not spoken. Richard turned to him now.

"Tommy is right," Jack said quietly. "My father said that if

Zachary was here today I was supposed to turn around and go right home. I'm glad he's not here, or I wouldn't get to play."

"Hey!" called the captain of the other team. "Are we going to play ball or what?"

"We're almost ready!" Richard called back. He turned back to his teammates. "So, who is going to hurl today?"

They chose Louis Leemer to take Zach's place on the pitching mound. They would be short one player in the outfield. They scattered to take their positions.

Louis leaned on his knees to study the first batter. Behind him at second base, Richard's stomach was sinking. He recognized this batter. Louis would not be able to get anything past him. Instinctively, Richard backed up a few steps.

Louis let the first pitch go. It was so far out of the strike zone that the other team burst into laughter.

"It's okay, Louis, just keep your focus," Richard called out. He clapped his hands in encouragement.

Louis wound up again. The pitch was straight this time, but not very fast. The batter had plenty of time to get a good look at it and swing hard. And that is exactly what he did. He whacked the ball right over Richard's head and into left field. Tommy Landers scrambled after it. By the time he chased it through the grass and heaved it to the infield, the batter was standing on second base, grinning at Richard.

Louis looked lost. Richard went to the mound to speak to him.

"It's just one hit, Louis," he said. "It's just the first inning."

"I'm not a hurler," Louis moaned.

"You've got a great arm," Richard said.

"For an outfielder," Louis responded. "I'm used to throwing the ball in from midfield."

"Take your time, Louis. Concentrate. You can do this."

Louis nodded. "Okay, let's go again."

The second batter came up to the plate. The runner took a generous lead off second base. It was as if he knew what would happen next. Louis only threw one pitch. The batter swung. Richard groaned. He could tell from the sound that the hit was a home run. The batter whooped his way to first base and then kept going. While the outfielders retrieved the ball, the two players from the Seventh Street Spades trotted around the diamond victoriously. The score was two to nothing, with no outs in the first inning.

Louis walked the next two batters, with eight very wide pitches in a row. Richard crouched in his position. There was still hope for a double play if the batter hit the ball to Tony. Tony could snap the ball to Richard on second, who would throw it to Jack Hammond. It would all happen in one smooth motion they had practiced a hundred times.

But the next ball did not come to shortstop. It went to right field. The runner on second base scored easily, and now there were runners on first base and third base—and still no outs. Richard sighed. Three to nothing. This was going to be a long game. He had looked forward to this game for weeks. They had almost three dozen people watching them play. And they were getting killed in the first inning.

Louis walked another batter. The bases were full.

Richard put his hand up for a time out. The team gathered on the pitcher's mound.

"We have to help Louis out here," Richard said.

"You mean we have to get him out of there," Tony said.

"That's exactly right," Richard said. He took the ball from Louis, who was relieved, and slapped it into Tony's hand. "You're the pitcher now."

"But who's going to play shortstop? What about the double play ball?"

"Look, you're used to throwing at me and hitting the mark

in double plays. You have to do the same thing throwing at the plate. Louis can cover second, and I'll play short."

"It seems to me that we need help in the outfield," Tommy said. "That's where all the hits are going."

Richard shook his head. "Not anymore, right, Tony? From now on, the ball doesn't leave the infield."

Tony nodded seriously.

"But the bases are full," Tommy reminded everyone, "with no outs. We've got to watch the play at the plate."

"Come on," chided the captain of the Seventh Street Spades. "Are you going to play or not?"

The boys on the Spades howled with laughter. "Maybe they're too weak from their desk jobs," one of them said. "Baseball is too much like physical labor. You actually have to move your muscles to play."

"That must be it!" another one scoffed. "They're in no condition to play against a union team."

Elton snapped his head around to Richard. "Are you going to let them get away with saying that?"

"The only thing to do," Richard said calmly, "is to pull ourselves together and prove we're the great team we know we are."

On the bench along the first-base line, Anna wondered what Richard was talking about with the rest of the team. Clearly they were in a lot of trouble. She saw Richard move the ball from Louis to Tony. But she also knew that no one was as good as Zachary. They needed Zach more today than they ever had before.

"Hit ball," Kjersten said. "Boy hit ball."

"That's right," Anna said. "We just didn't want so many boys to hit the ball."

"Hit ball," came the snickering voices behind them.

Anna turned around and glared at Martha again. Martha laughed aloud.

"You're sitting with a scab," Martha said loudly. "Did you know that, Anna Allerton? You're sitting with a scab. I saw her father driving a streetcar yesterday."

Anna glanced at Kjersten. "Is that true, Kjersten? Is your father driving a streetcar?"

"Drive? Ja, Papa drive."

So it was true. Mr. Olsson was driving one of those empty streetcars rattling around town.

It was all Anna could do to keep from turning around and shouting back at Martha Wilkerson. But it would do no good, and Anna did not want to hurt Kjersten's feelings. She glanced at Kjersten's face. Her new friend did not look as excited as she had a few minutes earlier. *She understands,* Anna thought, *she understands what Martha is saying and what those other girls are doing.*

The game had to get better. Anna could not imagine that it could be any worse.

Tony got ready to throw his first pitch. He took a long time, and he looked over his shoulder at Richard two times. Finally, he threw the ball. It was a good pitch—right into the strike zone. The batter let it pass. But at least Tony Tubiera had thrown the first strike of the game.

Richard sighed in relief. If only Tony could do that a few more times. Once again, Tony got ready to hurl the ball. Another strike! The Seventh Street team had stopped laughing.

On Tony's third pitch, the batter swung. It was a weak hit and took a long time to dribble to shortstop. Richard fielded it easily, but it was too late to throw it to home plate. He had to settle for throwing the ball to Jack at first base. One run scored, and the other runners advanced. But at least there was one out. The score was four to nothing, with runners on second and third.

The next batter got a good hit. Both runners scored, and the batter ended up on second base. Six to nothing. Then Tony struck out a batter. It took eight pitches, but he did it. Two out.

Richard just wanted the inning to be over. They were down by six runs, but it was only the first inning. The Spitfires had some good hitters on their team. If they could just get a chance to bat, they might be able to even the score.

Glancing across the field, Richard was sure he saw Zachary leaning against the fence with his hands stuffed in his pockets.

By the time the inning was over, the Seventh Street team led by eight runs. Now Richard just wanted the game to be over.

CHAPTER 7

A Fight in the Family

"I'm so glad you stopped by, Tina," Mama said. She poured three cups of tea, one for herself, one for Aunt Tina, and one for Anna. Mama usually did not include Anna in the grown-up tea talks. Anna was going to be on her best behavior so Mama would do it again sometime.

"Easter is just a few days away," Mama said. "We need to make plans for dinner after church."

"It's my turn to have the family over," Aunt Tina said. She dropped a sugar cube into her tea.

"Are you sure?" Mama asked. "I would be happy to have Easter dinner here."

"Nonsense," Aunt Tina said. "You've had the last two birthday parties. Let me do it."

Anna did not care where Easter dinner would be. But she did care what they would eat and hoped it would be something she could help prepare. Anna sat down at the kitchen table next to her mother and across from Aunt Tina. Richard was at the end of the table. Mama had not offered him any tea. Anna knew he would not drink it, anyway.

"Can we have that currant glaze on the ham?" Richard asked.

"Do you mean the one that Alison makes?" Mama asked.

"That's the one. I love that glaze!" Richard smacked his lips.

"I'm sure she will be willing to make the glaze—just for you."

"I'll get the ham, of course," Aunt Tina said, "and the sweet potatoes."

"What will we make, Mama?" Anna asked.

"What would you like to make?"

"Pies," Anna answered. "I want to learn to make a good pie crust."

"Ugh!" Richard groaned. "Do you have to experiment on the rest of us?"

"Hush, Richard," Mama said. "Your sister is turning into a fine cook. You should be glad to have her around. I know I am."

Anna beamed.

"What kind of pies?" Aunt Tina asked.

"Peach, apple, strawberry, cherry." Anna listed all her favorites.

Mama chuckled. "We'll see what kind of fruit preserves we have in the cellar."

"Can we use Pillsbury's Best Flour for the crust?" Anna asked.

"Of course. How could we live in Minneapolis and not buy the best flour in the country?"

"Where's Enoch?" Mama asked. "Maybe he has some suggestions for the menu."

"He's in the living room going over some papers," Aunt Tina said. "If we ask him what he'd like, the list will be far too long to accomplish."

Mama laughed.

A knock on the front door brought the menu planning to a halt.

"Richard, please go see who that is," Mama said.

He darted off to answer the door. Anna cocked her ear toward the voices that drifted into the kitchen from the hallway.

"It's the Fisks!" Anna said excitedly. "I wonder if Teddy is with them." Anna slid out of her chair.

Mama glanced at Aunt Tina. "I'm sorry, Tina, I had no idea they would be coming by."

"It's all right. You didn't know Enoch and I would drop in, either. We're all here. I'm sure everything will be fine."

Aunt Alison appeared in the doorway. Her seven-year-old son Theodore was right behind her.

"Is Charles with you?" Mama asked.

Aunt Alison looked over her shoulder nervously. "I left him in the living room with Enoch and Richard."

"Have Enoch and Charles seen each other lately?"

Aunt Alison and Aunt Tina both shook their heads emphatically.

"Then they'll have a lot to catch up on," Mama said optimistically.

Anna was not so sure it was a good idea to leave Uncle Charles and Uncle Enoch in the same room.

"What do you have to eat?" Teddy demanded.

"Theodore!" his mother scolded.

"I'm sorry. Cousin Marcia, might I have a bit of a snack?"

Mama smiled. "Such a little gentleman. Of course you may

have a snack. Anna, why don't you see what we have."

Anna got up and went to the icebox. "How about leftover chicken?" she suggested.

"White meat or dark?" he asked suspiciously.

"It's a leg."

"Good. I'll take that."

"Teddy," his mother coaxed.

"Thank you, Anna, I would like the chicken leg," Teddy said.

"We were just discussing Easter dinner," Mama said. "Tina has offered to have everyone at her house. And Richard has put in a request for your currant glaze."

Aunt Alison sighed and glanced toward the door that led to the living room. "A family dinner would be nice. We haven't done that for a long time."

Anna put the chicken leg on a plate and set it in front of Teddy. Aunt Alison had a strange look on her face.

"What is it, Alison?" Mama asked.

Aunt Alison hesitated. She glanced at Aunt Tina.

"It's all right," Aunt Tina said. "I can see that you're nervous about Charles and Enoch being together. To be honest, I am, too."

"I hate to create a situation where they might quarrel," Aunt Alison said.

"But we can't stop bringing the family together because Charles and Enoch don't agree on unions and management. Charles and Enoch have known each other a long time. I believe they are genuinely fond of each other."

"I'm sure they are, too," Aunt Alison said. "And they both love you, Tina. But lately Charles is so edgy about this union business. I can't predict how he will behave."

"They seem to be doing just fine right now," Mama said. "You left Charles in the living room with Enoch, and we haven't heard a peep out of them."

"That's not necessarily good," Aunt Alison said. "It means they're not speaking to each other at all."

Just then, Richard entered the kitchen. He slumped into a chair.

"I'd rather listen to you talk about recipes," he said, "than sit in there with the two of them."

"What's going on?"

"Nothing. That's the problem. They're just sitting there staring at each other. Uncle Enoch pretends to be working on his papers, but I don't think he really is. And Uncle Charles is making me crazy, jiggling his leg all the time."

"Jiggling his leg?" his wife said in alarm. "That means there is something on his mind." She turned to Richard. "Didn't he say anything at all?"

Richard shrugged. "He asked me about my baseball team. But I don't think he heard a word I said."

"Is he twitching his moustache?" Teddy asked, his mouth full of chicken.

Richard nodded.

Teddy and Aunt Alison looked at each other.

"Papa's going to be angry, isn't he?" Teddy said what they were all thinking.

Just at that moment, the voices in the next room exploded. Anna's heart raced as she jumped out of her chair. Richard was ahead of her, bounding into the living room. Mama and the other women were right behind them. They stood at the edge of the living room. The men seemed not to notice anyone had entered the room.

"You're an intelligent man, Charles," Uncle Enoch was saying. "I do not understand why you are behaving like such a simpleton on this matter."

The color was rising in Uncle Charles's face. "You see the world one way, Enoch, and I see it another way."

"You see the world the way you want to see it," his brother-in-law retorted. "You want the unions to be powerful, so you inflame the average person. You fill their heads with ideas that can never come true."

"The unions will make their ideas come true—and life will be better for the average worker."

Uncle Enoch slapped the table next to his chair. Anna jumped back.

"When will you understand that the people who own these businesses have something to say on these questions?" he shouted. "You want to create a perfect world for the average worker, but you want the owners to pay for it—men like Charles Pillsbury and Thomas Lowry. They've worked hard to build up their businesses."

"They've made themselves rich by keeping their workers in poverty!" Uncle Charles stood up and towered over Uncle Enoch.

"Mama?" Anna whispered. "Shouldn't we do something?"

"I'm not sure what to do," Mama answered.

"Don't do anything," Aunt Tina said. "Charles and Enoch are grown men. Eventually they have to work this out."

Richard was not convinced. "What if they don't?"

Esther tumbled down the stairs from her room just then and ran to her mother. "Mama, why are they yelling?"

Uncle Enoch pushed his papers aside and pulled himself out of his chair. He was not as tall as Charles, and his cork leg made him unsteady for a moment. But he stared up at his opponent and continued his side of the argument. His jaw was set, and his words were clipped.

"Am I to believe that you think getting no pay at all is better for those workers than the pay Mr. Lowry offers?"

"The wage cut is only part of it. The strikers are standing on a principle, Enoch."

"And their children are going hungry for the sake of that principle," retorted Uncle Enoch. "Does the principle justify the way they terrorize the new drivers or the way they taunt anyone who tries to ride a streetcar?"

"They are doing what they believe they must do."

"And what if they are wrong?"

The front door opened and Papa came in. Instinctively Anna flew across the room and snuggled against him.

Papa put down his medical bag next to the door and looked around the living room.

"What in the world is going on in here?" Papa demanded. "I could hear you halfway down the block."

The two men did not answer. They continued to glare at each other.

"Don't bother to answer," Papa said, "because there is no good answer. There is no excuse for the way you two are behaving. I don't care what is going on in the streets, and I don't care what the politicians are saying. You will not bring your arguments into my home."

Uncle Charles broke his stare and turned to Papa. "I'm sorry, Daniel. Of course you are right. We let things get out of hand."

But Papa was not finished. "Charles, Enoch is married to your sister. I would think that out of respect for Tina, you would make an effort to be civil to him. And you, too, Enoch. Do not forget that Charles is Tina's brother."

"You are quite right, of course," Uncle Enoch said. He turned around and picked up his papers. "Tina, I believe we should leave now." He moved toward the door without so much as glancing at his brother-in-law.

Anna watched Aunt Tina's face. Whatever she was thinking or feeling, she did not show anything in her face. Aunt Tina turned to Mama and Aunt Alison.

"I'll telephone you," she said. "We'll finish making our

plans for Easter dinner over the phone."

"Are you sure we should get together?" Aunt Alison whispered, glancing up at her husband. "It could be very unpleasant."

Tina kept her voice even. "Easter Sunday celebrates the resurrection of our Lord—victory over sin. That includes family arguments. I will not let this union business destroy our family."

"Tina," Uncle Enoch called urgently as he opened the front door.

"Don't forget the glaze, Alison," she said as she headed for the door.

As soon as the couple had gone, Uncle Charles said, "Alison, perhaps we ought to be on our way as well. We only meant to stop in for a moment."

"Yes, of course," she replied. "I'll just get Teddy."

In another moment, they were gone as well.

Anna looked up at Papa. "Will Uncle Charles and Uncle Enoch be friends again?" she asked. "When the strike is settled, will they stop fighting?"

Papa sighed. "I hope they stop fighting no matter what happens with the strike. They are both bigger and stronger than this petty arguing."

"But they don't think it's petty," Richard said. "They're on opposite sides, and they both think they're right."

"Then we must help them to see the truth," Papa said. "Both Mr. Lowry and the unions have some good arguments. They have to learn to listen to each other—and that includes Enoch and Charles."

CHAPTER 8

Lost!

"Can we go? Can we go?" Eight-year-old Esther twirled to make her new pink Easter dress spin.

"What's your hurry?" Richard asked. "Easter dinner is not for two more hours."

"I want to play with Teddy," Esther said.

"Be careful of your new dress," Mama said. "Perhaps you should take an old frock along to play in later."

"No!" protested Esther. "I want to keep my new dress on. I've hardly worn it at all—just to church this morning." Esther twirled around the kitchen. The wide skirt of her new pink cotton dress spun in a perfect circle.

"Everyone looked beautiful in church today," Anna said. "Cousin Judith should always wear that color green. And Polly looked so wonderful sitting next to her beau."

Mama took a pie from the oven and set it on the counter. "Esther, please stop spinning. You're going to knock something over."

"I'm being careful!" Esther protested.

Mama warned her with a raised eyebrow and Esther screeched to a halt.

Anna gently touched the top of the pie, testing for doneness.

"Mmmm," Richard said, smacking his lips. "Maybe we should have a snack now."

"Don't you touch my pie!" Anna said.

"It looks perfect, Anna," Mama said. "You should be proud of yourself."

Anna was proud. "Let me wrap it up, Mama," she said as she pulled open a cupboard and reached for a towel. "I want to carry it to the Stevensons'.."

"Mama, is Teddy really going to be there?" Esther asked.

"Of course he is. The whole family will be there."

"Everyone?"

"Everyone. The Fisks, the Stevensons, everyone."

"Even Uncle Charles?"

"Why, of course Charles will be there."

Esther stuck her lower lip out thoughtfully. "Teddy's family did not sit in front of us today at church. They always sit in the row in front of us."

Mama started wrapping up a basket of biscuits. "Church was very crowded today because it was Easter. Teddy's family had to find a seat in the back."

"No, they didn't," Esther said. "They were there early. I saw them. Teddy said his father did not want to sit near Uncle Enoch."

Anna watched Mama carefully. How would she explain why the two men were angry with each other?

"What else does Teddy say?" Mama asked casually. She laid a linen napkin over the top of the biscuit basket.

"He says that his papa says Uncle Enoch doesn't understand about the streetcar strike. He says Uncle Enoch is being too stubborn for his own good."

Mama nodded. "Yes, that's what Charles thinks."

"Is he right, Mama?" Esther genuinely wanted to know.

"It's very complicated, Esther. Why don't we talk about it another time? But I promise you that Teddy will be there today, and you can play with him all afternoon."

"Then let's go!" Esther cried.

"I believe we are ready!" Mama said enthusiastically.

Anna's stomach was a little bit nervous. If her two older cousins sat down at the same table, how long would the family dinner last? Aunt Tina had a long table, and there would be fourteen people there—fifteen if Polly brought her new beau. Uncle Charles and Uncle Enoch would not even have to talk to each other. But would they be able to control themselves? Would they want to?

Mama and Esther were ready to go.

"Shouldn't we wait for Papa?" Anna asked.

Mama shook her head. "He had to see a patient at the hospital. I told him just to meet us at the Stevensons'."

"I suppose it would be silly for him to come all the way back here first," Anna said. She buttoned her new sapphire cloak under her neck.

"Especially with no streetcars running," Richard added.

They gathered their things and started out. Anna carried the cherry pie, while Mama carried the apple pie and corn pudding. Esther had the biscuits. Richard lugged a sack of potatoes destined to be peeled, boiled, and mashed at the Stevensons' house.

As they walked, Esther chattered about her new dress and the new wooden top that she carried in her pocket to show

Teddy. Anna concentrated on keeping the cherry pie level. Even through the thick towel she had wrapped around the pie plate, she could feel the oven's warmth and smell the sweet cherry filling. Her stomach growled.

Richard scanned the neighborhood. "A lot of people are out walking today," he observed. "Most people stay home on Sunday afternoons."

Anna could see that Richard was right. A lot of people were in the streets. "Maybe they are out for the same reason we are," she said. "Waiting for their Easter dinner."

Richard squeezed his eyebrows together. "I don't think so. They're not carrying food. And most of them are not really walking. They're just standing around."

Once again, Richard was right. Anna was starting to feel nervous.

"Mama?" she said quietly.

"I'm sure everything is fine," Mama said. "People are a bit restless with the strike, that's all."

Anna was not convinced. She looked at Richard. He seemed to be watching the street carefully.

"We're walking too slow," Esther announced, paying no attention to the conversation. She proceeded to skip.

"Esther," Mama warned. "Don't get too far ahead of me."

"Here comes a streetcar," Esther said, pointing.

The car was empty, of course. Anna could see straight through it. The car was headed toward downtown.

"Isn't that Kjersten's father?" Richard asked.

"Where?" Anna's eyes darted through the crowd.

"In the streetcar," Richard said. "I think he was driving."

The car stopped at the next corner, and an elderly woman boarded. Immediately two young men swung aboard. Even from down the block, Anna could hear them heckling the driver.

"Scab!"

"Management sympathizer!"

The car rumbled down the street. Anna could see the two young men hovering over the driver. At the next stop, the elderly passenger got off.

"She's an old lady," Richard said, disgusted. "Why don't they leave her alone and let her ride?"

"Do you really think that was Kjersten's father?" Anna asked.

"I didn't get a good look," Richard said, "and I've only seen her father once. But she told you he had started driving streetcars."

"Do you think we could catch up with it?"

"Now, Anna," Mama said, "I understand your concern about your friend's father. But you cannot put yourself in danger. He made his own choice to drive a streetcar."

"I just want to know if it was him."

The car had stopped again, three blocks up. Anna peered down the street, trying to focus on the driver's profile.

"Esther!" Mama called. "Wait for me."

Anna did not turn around at her mother's voice. Why couldn't Esther just be patient and walk with the rest of the family?

Try as she might, Anna could not see the driver clearly. He was too far away.

"I can't see him," she said, disappointed. No one answered her.

Now she whirled around. Where was Mama? And Esther and Richard?

In the last few minutes, the street had flooded with dozens of people. Where had they all come from? And what were they doing? They seemed to move like the current of the Mississippi River toward downtown Minneapolis. Caught up in the pressure of the growing crowd, Anna stumbled along for a few feet, clutching her still-warm pie. She examined the crowd for her mother's bright blue shawl or Esther's new pink dress. They were nowhere to be seen.

"Richard!" she cried aloud. "Mama!" Anna could feel tears of panic springing to her eyes.

A couple people passing by turned to glance at her. But there was no flicker of recognition in their eyes. They were strangers.

Stay calm, Anna told herself. *They can't have gone far. You only turned your head for a moment.*

Against her will, Anna was moving down the street with the flow of the crowd. Cradling her pie, she pressed her way out of the mainstream. Mama always told her that if she got lost, she should stay where she was and someone would find her. She was lost now. Anna determined to get out of the crowd and stay put.

Anna pressed herself up against a fence. She recognized the well-tended home before her. It was Martha Wilkerson's house. The picket at the top of the fence was poking into Anna's back. But she hardly felt it. She poured all her energy into looking for her family in the throbbing mob.

The murmurs of the crowd had swelled to a roar. Mumblings had become shouts. Anna could hear what the people were saying.

"We'll teach them a lesson they won't forget!"

"We'll show that Thomas Lowry that he needs us more than he thinks he does."

"We have to get rid of those scabs."

Get rid of the scabs? What do they mean? Anna wondered.

Three men charged down the middle of the street, shoulder to shoulder, marching in step.

Over the noise of the crowd, Anna cried out, "Mama! Richard!"

"Anna!"

Relief swept over Anna at the sound of her brother's voice. "I'm here, Richard, here!"

She still could not see him.

"I'm coming!"

And then he was there.

"What happened?" Anna asked.

Richard shook his head. "I'm not sure. Mama chased after Esther, and when we turned around, you were gone."

"But I didn't go anywhere!"

"Never mind. I found you."

"But where are Mama and Esther?"

The crowd around them thickened by the moment. Dozens had turned into hundreds, perhaps even thousands.

"I've never seen so many people," Richard said, "except at the ballpark or a parade."

"Richard, where are Mama and Esther?" Anna said again, more urgently this time.

Richard turned to look at his sister and sighed. "I don't know."

"Are they waiting for you somewhere?"

"I don't know. Mama was worried about you, and I said I would find you. And now—"

"And now it will be impossible to find them."

"Let's not give up yet," Richard said. Anna could see the concentration in his dark eyes. "We haven't even started looking yet."

Anna swallowed a sob. "I never did like crowds," she said.

Still carrying the sack of potatoes, Richard offered his elbow. "Here, hang on to me. Whatever you do, don't let go."

"Believe me, I won't!"

"Let's go back to the corner where you saw the streetcar," Richard suggested. "That's the last place we were all together."

Anna thought that was a good idea. But it was harder than it sounded. Everyone else was swarming down the street in the other direction. With one hand, she held her prized pie. With the other hand, she squeezed Richard's elbow. Together, they forged their way against the ever-growing stream.

Men of all ages filled the street, and women and children, too. The men marched with determination toward a goal that Anna could not see. The children whooped and hollered. Anna heard the edge of her new cloak rip when someone pulled on it. She jerked herself away and held onto Richard's arm more tightly.

"Richard, what are all these people doing?"

"What did you say?" Richard shouted. It was getting harder to hear each other.

"I said, what are all these people doing?"

Richard shook his head in confusion.

"Do you think Mama and Esther are all right?" Anna asked anxiously.

They had arrived at the corner where they had seen the streetcar. There was hardly room to stand. Hundreds of people flooded the intersection. But there was no sign of a bright blue shawl or a new pink dress.

"Richard, what if we don't find them?" Anna said. "Mama always says to stay put when you get lost."

"We can't stay here," Richard said. "Even Mama would say that this is dangerous."

Anna's heart raced. Where was Mama?

"We have to get out of the way of this mob," Richard said.

"But what about Mama and Esther?" Anna pleaded.

Richard hesitated only a moment before answering. "Mama will do whatever she has to do to keep Esther safe. And she would want us to keep ourselves safe."

Anna nodded. Richard was right. "But where will we go?"

CHAPTER 9

The Easter Riot

"Come on," Richard said, "this way."

"Where are we going?" Anna asked.

Richard must not have heard her. He did not answer. Anna held on to his arm a little tighter. She thought how silly they must look carrying a sack of potatoes and a cherry pie through the mob.

Anna realized Richard was leading her straight into the heart of the crowd.

"What are you doing?" she cried out. She tugged on his elbow.

Richard shouted over his shoulder, "Trust me."

Anna got bumped from the back. The cherry pie started to

slide. She jerked her arm from Richard's elbow and gripped the pie more securely with both hands.

Richard turned around to see what had happened. "I told you not to let go of me."

"I'm sorry. The pie started to fall."

"Forget about the pie." Whatever calm Richard had managed to hang on to was disappearing. His dark eyes darted back and forth, alert to every movement of the crowd.

Anna took Richard's elbow again, but she kept her grip on the pie. They were carried along by the crowd until they came to the next corner. Richard steered them down a side street. They rested against a brick building.

Anna swallowed nervously.

"We have to figure out what we're going to do," Richard said, breathing heavily.

Anna watched the crowd around them and wished she were somewhere else, anywhere else. She kept looking for Mama and Esther. Everything looked brown and gray. Nothing was blue or pink.

"We should keep going to the Stevensons'," Anna suggested. "Everyone will expect us there."

Richard shook his head. "It's too far—at least another mile."

"But Mama will go there."

"I'm not sure what Mama will do. If she's trapped in the crowd like we are, she won't be able to get to the Stevensons', either."

"We could go home. It's closer."

"We'd have to go against the crowd," Richard said.

That seemed like an impossible task.

"We'll take the back streets," Anna said. But even the back streets were filling up.

"I know!" Richard said suddenly. "The hospital. It's only a few blocks from here."

"Yes, and Papa might still be there."

"Even if he's not, we could use a telephone."

"All right, let's do it."

With new determination, they turned to join the still-swelling crowd.

"Richard, how many people do you think are here?"

"Must be thousands," Richard answered. "They just keep coming. The crowd goes on for blocks and blocks."

They walked a block toward the hospital. It seemed to Anna that they were going only a few inches at a time. It was hard to keep the pie level. Cherry filling had started to seep through the towel wrapped around the pie tin. It stuck to Anna's hand and dampened her sapphire clothing, turning a deep purple. It reminded her of blood. She shivered involuntarily.

They came to a standstill, pressed in on every side.

"What's happening, Richard?" Anna shouted. She could hardly breathe. "I can't see."

A tall man next to her leaned toward Anna. "I'll tell you what's happening. We're going to teach that Thomas Lowry a lesson once and for all. You can be proud to be here today. This will be a day Minneapolis will not soon forget."

Anna did not answer the man. Without looking up at him, she moved even closer to Richard.

Richard was craning his neck, trying to see through the crowd.

"I think there's a streetcar up there," he said. "I saw it a minute ago, but I can't see it anymore."

Anna was just too short. She could not see anything. A jolt from behind pushed her into the woman in front of her. The pie oozed some more.

"Wait!" Richard cried. "The streetcar is still there. It's just covered with people."

"People are riding the streetcar?"

"No, they're climbing all over it."

"Climbing?"

"Yes, standing on top of it, hanging out the windows."

Anna's stomach was flipping. "Richard, I'm scared."

Then she remembered the streetcar they had seen earlier. "Richard! Is it the same streetcar we saw earlier?"

"Probably. There haven't been any others going by."

"Kjersten's father! What if that was Kjersten's father driving the streetcar?"

Richard was silent.

"Richard, we have to find out!"

"I never said I was sure it was him. It just looked like him. It could have been another Swedish immigrant."

"Or it could have been Mr. Olsson."

"We don't know that for sure."

"You're the one who thought it was him!"

"I was probably wrong," Richard insisted. He pushed Anna in front of him and pointed through an opening in the crowd. "Look, see for yourself what is happening."

The crowd had parted just enough for Anna to spot the streetcar. Men, women, and children of all ages were scrambling up the sides of the car and hoisting themselves to the top. Those on top offered their hands to pull more people to the top of the car. Anna could not imagine how there was room for one more person up there. Still they climbed.

"I don't see any horses to pull the car," Anna observed.

Richard stood on his tiptoes and craned his neck. "I don't, either. They must have unhitched them."

A man with a bullhorn leaned out the side of the car.

"Thomas Lowry, if you are out there," he shouted, "take note. You cannot ignore us. You cannot simply hire more drivers. What will happen when you have no more streetcars?"

"What does he mean, Richard?" Anna asked.

71

"Anna, I think we have to get out of here. Now!" Richard pulled Anna forcefully along. She stumbled as she tried to keep her balance. "We have to get to the hospital."

But to get to the hospital, they had to pass the streetcar. Richard wound his way steadily through the crowd.

"People are getting out now," Anna said as they got closer to the streetcar.

"Don't pay any attention," Richard said. "Concentrate on the hospital."

"But why are they getting out? Are they finished?"

"How would I know?" Richard snapped. "I just want to get out of here."

"But, Richard—"

Richard spun around. His mouth opened to speak, but then he saw what Anna was looking at. A row of men had lined themselves up along one side of the streetcar. Bracing their feet solidly, they leaned into the car. It rocked from side to side. Whooping, more men joined the effort. Dozens were pushing on the side of the streetcar. The car rocked some more. They pushed again. Now the car was tipping.

Instinctively, Richard jerked Anna back. The car tumbled over on one side. With a mighty groan, the joints on one end gave way, and the top of the car splintered off. A wheel broke loose and skidded through the crowd. Once again, the mob scrambled to stand on top of the wreckage. In only a few seconds, it was impossible to see what they were standing on. A mountain of people had arisen in the middle of Minneapolis. The horses had been unhitched. Now they thundered down the street, whinnying and thrashing their hooves. The crowd parted to let them pass. No one tried to catch the frightened animals.

"You are destroying private property!" The shout came from the middle of the street. Four men, their fists raised in the air, charged toward the buried streetcar.

The man with the bullhorn laughed roughly. "If you are Mr. Lowry's men, you are too late."

"Have you no respect for something that doesn't belong to you?"

"Just like Mr. Lowry respects us, eh? He thinks he owns us. Well, he doesn't. He won't even come to the arbitration table. When will he show us the respect we deserve?"

Lowry's men hurled themselves toward the man with the bullhorn. He toppled over backward. Anna could hear fists smacking flesh. Blood spattered faces and clothing. The mob on the top of the streetcar moved like an avalanche down to the street. It was too late for words. Fists were swinging in every direction.

"Anna, we have to get out of here now!" Richard shouted. He took firm hold of her arm and pulled her along.

Suddenly a man in a brown coat fell backward right into Richard. Richard lost his balance—and his grip on Anna—and was swallowed up into the mob. His sack of potatoes hit the ground and split open. Seizing the opportunity, some teenagers scrambled to pick up the potatoes and began heaving them into the crowd.

Still clutching her crumbling pie, Anna searched for Richard. Everything was happening so fast! The crowd swirled around her. Anna was getting dizzy and was afraid she would fall down, too.

"Richard!"

"Anna!" came the muffled response.

"Richard, where are you?"

Then she spotted his boots. Richard was sprawled across the middle of the street. In their rush to join the fracas, people were stepping on him or stepping over him. No one stopped to help him. Anna forced her way into the flow of traffic and jerked to a stop in front of Richard. A woman hurtling past knocked the pie out of Anna's arms. The pie landed upside down. Cherries oozed through the towel. Then someone stepped on the pie tin, smashing it beyond repair.

"My pie!" Anna moaned.

Richard was on his feet. "Forget the pie."

"Richard, are you all right?" Anna examined her brother. She saw footmarks on his jacket, and his face was bruised. Blood trickled from a cut on his left cheek.

"I don't think it's anything serious," Richard said, "but I'm glad we're headed to the hospital."

"I wish Mama was here," Anna moaned.

"I just hope Mama and Esther are all right."

With their elbows linked, they started off again. Inch by inch, they edged their way to the outskirts of the crowd. Finally the hospital building was in sight. But Anna knew it would take them a long time to go even a few blocks.

Whoever had been driving the streetcar had long ago abandoned it. Anna found herself scanning the faces in the crowd, looking to see if Mr. Olsson was there.

Tripping and jostling their way through the crowd, Richard and Anna made slow but steady progress. When they reached the hospital door, Richard pushed it open and they tumbled in.

CHAPTER 10
At the Hospital

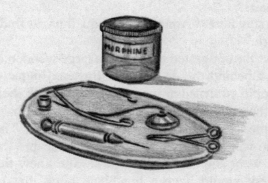

Inside the main hospital door, Richard and Anna stopped for a moment to catch their breath. They dropped into a pair of empty wooden chairs away from the door.

"Are you all right, Richard?" Anna asked. "You look pale."

Richard raised one hand to the side of his head. "I have an awful headache. I think I got kicked."

"I couldn't even see what happened to you," Anna said.

"I got knocked over, that's all. I should have been paying better attention to what was happening."

"Don't be silly," Anna said. "You couldn't help what happened."

Richard leaned his head back against the wall behind him and closed his eyes.

"Maybe you need a doctor," Anna said. "The cut on your cheek is still bleeding." She reached into the pocket of her pastel plaid skirt for a handkerchief and dabbed at the cut.

"I'll be all right," Richard responded, wincing a little bit. "But we should try to find out if Papa is still here."

Anna surveyed the lobby. It was crowded. Richard and Anna were not the only ones who had come to the hospital to escape the chaos of the streets. They had gotten the last two empty chairs.

"You stay here," Anna said, "and I'll try to find out if Papa is still here."

Across the congested room was a large wooden desk painted green, and behind the desk was a flustered nurse. Nearly two dozen people swarmed around her trying to ask their questions. Some of them were scraped and bruised and probably wanted a doctor. Others were just asking a lot of questions. The nurse kept looking down the hall as if she wanted to escape.

Anna went and stood at the desk. She knew that the nurse at that desk would have a big black book that would show whether her father had signed out and left the hospital. Ordinarily it was a simple thing to approach the desk and ask about Papa. But Anna could not get anywhere near the desk that day. The nurse would not pay attention to a small ten year old when twenty adults were pressing in on her. Anna tried to figure out if there was a line so she could get in it. Three times she was pushed away by someone much bigger than she.

Finally she turned back to Richard. He had not moved the whole time she was gone.

"The nurse is too busy," Anna reported. "I think I'll go up to the ward on the third floor. That's where Papa usually sees his patients. You can stay here."

"No," Richard said, "we should stay together."

Inwardly Anna was relieved Richard wanted to stay with her.

Richard pulled himself to his feet, and they started down the hall to find the dark stairs that would take them to the third floor. At the top of the stairs they turned left and continued on to the ward. Richard cautiously pushed open the door to the large room. Sixteen beds were arranged in neat rows down both sides of the ward. Several nurses made their way swiftly from one bed to the next to make sure the patients were comfortable.

"I don't see Papa," Anna announced.

"I don't, either," Richard said. "Where else should we look?"

"We can check the other wards," Anna said.

"You'll do no such thing!" barked a voice behind them.

Richard and Anna spun around to find the ward's head nurse scowling down at them.

"This is a hospital, not a playground," she said.

"We're looking for Dr. Allerton," Richard said. "He's our father."

"I'm aware of that, but children do not belong in a hospital ward."

"We have to find him," Anna said.

"There!" The nurse pointed to a small, dark room across the hall. "You may wait there. When I see Dr. Allerton, I will tell him where to find you."

"My brother is hurt," Anna said. "He needs to see a doctor."

The nurse narrowed her eyes and studied Richard's face. In the same harsh tone, she said, "That's a nasty cut. I'll send in a cold pack. But you must wait in there!" She pointed emphatically to the small room. Richard and Anna shuffled across the hall reluctantly.

The room was furnished with four wooden chairs and a small table. A round window high in the wall provided the only light.

"Do you think she will really tell Papa we're here?" Anna asked.

"I hope so," Richard answered. "And I hope she sends that cold pack."

"Does your head hurt very much?" Anna asked softly.

Richard nodded.

They waited in that room for what seemed like hours. Richard laid his head down on the table. Anna shuffled to the doorway and looked out. The third floor seemed much busier than it usually was. Nurses moved down the hall with quick, purposeful steps. Their crisp uniforms swished and scratched with every step. Doctors in white jackets hung their stethoscopes around their necks and looked worried.

Suddenly Anna jumped out into the hall.

"Papa!"

"Anna! What are you doing here?"

Anna took her father's hand and pulled him into the small room.

"Richard! Are you all right?" Papa put his hand on Richard's flushed cheek.

"He got kicked in the head," Anna explained.

Then she told Papa the whole story of how the family had started out for the Stevensons' for Easter dinner and Mama and Esther had disappeared.

Papa made Richard sit up so he could look in his eyes.

"I don't see any sign of serious injury," Papa said.

"I just have a headache," Richard said. "I'll be all right. But what about Mama and Esther?"

"There's a telephone down at the end of the hall," Papa said. "We'll go call the Stevensons and see if they made it over there."

Mama and Esther were not at the Stevensons. No one but the Stevenson family was there. Aunt Tina had heard about the tipped-over streetcar and the riot. In fact, she told Papa that two streetcars had been tipped over, not just one. But she had not heard from Mama.

"That means they are still out there somewhere," Anna said.

"They could have gone in another building," Richard said.

Papa looked worried—very worried. "I want to look for them."

"But Papa, the riot!" Anna protested.

"I'll settle the two of you in a safe, quiet place. Richard, maybe we can find you a bed to rest on until your head stops hurting. Then I'm going to go out to look for your mother and sister."

"Dr. Allerton, come quick!" It was the head nurse. "They need you down on the first floor."

"What happened?"

"Several more men have just come in, and they are hurt quite badly."

Papa sighed. "All right, I'll be right there."

"Papa, don't leave us here," Anna pleaded.

"Come with me," Papa responded, "but stay out of the way. I don't want you to get hurt."

Papa thundered down the stairs. Anna and Richard did their best to keep up with him. Richard groaned with the jerking movement. The lobby was even more crowded than it had been earlier. Papa crossed a corner of the lobby and ducked into a room behind the main lobby.

Anna gasped when she saw the first patient.

"It's the man with the bullhorn!" she said to Richard.

"I don't think he thought anyone could hurt him," Richard said.

The man's left arm did not look right. The skin was scraped off one side of his face, and his right eye was bruised and swollen.

"What do you think happened to him?" Anna asked.

"It was probably those management men," Richard

answered. "Remember? The three men who ran up right after the streetcar fell over?"

Anna nodded. She remembered. "But there were only three of them—three against the whole crowd."

"They must have had other friends with them. Besides, with a baseball bat or a heavy stick, all it would take would be a couple of swings."

Anna grimaced at the picture Richard had created in her mind.

Being careful to stay out of the way, they watched their father at work. He set the broken arm and gave the nurses instructions about the other injuries.

"When can I get out of here, Doc?" the man asked.

"I'd like you to stay a couple days," Papa told the man.

"I can't do that. I have no money to pay you. I'm a street-car driver."

"We'll worry about that later," Papa said. "I think you have two broken ribs. You must be taken care of." He turned to the nurse. "Make sure he gets a bed in one of the wards."

"Here comes the next one," the nurse responded, as an orderly wheeled in another patient.

"I know this man," Papa said.

Anna's heart leaped. Mr. Olsson? She lurched forward for a better look. No, it was not Mr. Olsson.

"I've treated him before," Papa continued. "He's one of Thomas Lowry's managers."

"Then he's a dog!" growled the first patient.

"Orderly," Papa said, nodding his head at his first patient. "I think you can take him upstairs now."

"Dog, he's a dog!" shouted the man as the orderly wheeled him away.

Papa turned his attention to his new patient, who was unconscious. With a thumb, he pushed one of the man's eyelids open. "I don't like the way his pupils look," he told the nurse.

The nurse from the front desk stuck her head in the room. "Doctor, there are two more coming in now."

"Aren't there any other doctors around?" Papa asked.

"Dr. Harrison is upstairs with a critical patient. Dr. Norris is delivering a baby."

"Is there no one else?"

"It's Easter Sunday, Doctor," the nurse responded. "Most of the doctors did their rounds hours ago and went home to Easter dinner."

"We need help," Papa insisted. "Get on the telephone and call Dr. Madison and Dr. Scott. Now!"

"Yes, Doctor."

The man on the gurney before Papa began gasping for air. Papa held the man's mouth open and pushed down on his tongue with a flat wooden stick.

"His airway is blocked! We'll have to intubate!"

Nurse Hopkins flew into action and produced a narrow tube.

"Hold his mouth open," Papa ordered as he started forcing the tube down the man's mouth. The patient thrashed. Two more nurses came in to help hold him down. In another moment, Papa had the tube down his throat and the man was breathing steadily.

Anna could hardly watch. She scrunched up against the wall as tightly as she could. Richard had found a spot in the corner where he could sit down and lean his head against the wall.

Papa stepped back from his patient just as the orderlies brought in two more men.

"What do we have?" Papa asked.

The nurses gave the best report they could on the injuries they had observed. Blood and dangling bones filled the small room.

Richard and Anna pressed themselves up against the wall,

81

hardly able to take in what they were seeing.

"Doctor, perhaps your children would be more comfortable somewhere else," Nurse Hopkins suggested.

"No, they're fine," Papa said without looking up.

"It's okay, Papa," Anna said. "We can go wait in the lobby."

Papa glanced up for just a second. "Don't go anywhere else, do you understand? And if any fighting breaks out, you come right back in here?"

"Yes, Papa."

"Miss Hopkins, please make sure that my son has a place to sit down."

"Yes, Doctor."

Nurse Hopkins ushered Richard and Anna back out to the main lobby.

When they were alone in the crowded lobby, Richard said quietly, "They are all the same."

Anna turned to him, puzzled.

"When they are hurt," Richard said, "they are all the same. They need a doctor. They all have the same broken bones and bloody faces. And Papa helps them all. He doesn't care if they are union or management."

Anna scanned the lobby. Richard was right. Everyone was the same. She could not tell just by looking whether the woman in the green coat was waiting for a union husband or a management husband. She could not tell if the children playing in the corner belonged to a union father or a management father.

She found herself looking for Mr. Olsson once again and praying that he was safe.

CHAPTER 11

Where's Mama?

Richard's headache was getting better. The throbbing had lessened to a dull ache. Nurse Hopkins had cleaned the cut on his cheek and put a bandage on it. As long as he sat still, his ribs did not feel too sore.

In the lobby, Richard picked up a newspaper someone had abandoned. The headlines for Easter Sunday 1889 cried out: "Strike Continues. Lowry Says No Negotiations." "Restless Drivers Threaten Action." "Union Demands Heighten."

He scanned the beginning of one article: "Thomas Lowry, owner of the Minneapolis Streetcar Company, insists that he will not submit to arbitration to settle the streetcar strike. 'In the future,' said Lowry, 'the Minneapolis Street Railway will run its own business instead of having it run by a union.' Although the business has suffered greatly during the strike, Lowry continues to hire replacement drivers. He has brought in a hundred men from Kansas City to drive the routes abandoned by union drivers. If Lowry continues to refuse arbitration, drivers are threatening further action to force his cooperation."

Richard tossed the paper aside. The news was already old. The drivers were no longer threatening action. They had taken action that morning. Their action had brought Richard and his sister to the hospital lobby instead of to the Stevensons' house for a scrumptious Easter dinner. Richard's stomach was starting to growl. The better his head felt, the hungrier he got.

Where had Anna gone? Richard wondered, as he glanced at her tattered sapphire cloak on the empty chair beside him. They had promised Papa not to wander off. His eyes darted around the lobby, looking for his sister.

Anna had shuffled up to the big green desk. The lobby was just as full as it had been before, but the crowd seemed more organized. A different nurse was on duty. She seemed less flustered and more in control. "The line forms to the left," the nurse called out every few minutes. She answered questions and passed out forms for people to fill out. Every once in awhile, someone wanted to ask a question without waiting in line. But the nurse firmly said, "The line forms to the left."

Papa had been out to the lobby to check on Richard and Anna two times in the last two hours. No new emergencies had come in for more than an hour, and Dr. Norris and Dr. Madison had finally showed up to help Papa. Anna thought that things ought to be settling down. She wondered where Papa was now. She supposed he was at the bedside of the patient he had intubated. Papa had read a lot of articles about intubation before he ever tried it. But finally he was convinced that the only way to help some patients breathe was to intubate—to put a long tube down their throats so they could get air to their lungs. Then Papa would make sure the patient was all right and breathing on his own before he would relax.

Papa was a good doctor. Anna was sure of that. But she wanted to know how much longer the good doctor would have to stay at the hospital.

Anna eyed the long line at the green reception desk. She did not want to stand in that line just to ask if the nurse knew what her father was doing. How could that nurse know? She had been in the lobby the whole time. Anna inched toward the door that led to the examination room behind the lobby. Maybe Papa was still there.

As she got closer to the room, Anna cocked her ear. She did not hear any noises coming from the room. Probably all the patients had been moved to the wards, she thought. But she wanted to check the room just to be sure Papa was not there. With her hand on the doorknob, she turned to look around. She did not see Nurse Hopkins anywhere. Still with her back to the door, she turned the knob and leaned back on the door and pushed it open.

The clatter that followed told Anna that the room had not been empty. When she got the door open, she saw a dismayed Nurse Hopkins scrambling to pick up a tray. Medical instruments had scattered all over the floor.

The nurse scowled at Anna. "Look what you did!"

"I'm sorry," Anna exclaimed. "I'll help you pick everything up." She stooped to the floor and retrieved a pair of steel tongs.

"Don't touch anything," Miss Hopkins said. "Some of these are delicate instruments. Now they'll have to be cleaned all over again."

"I. . .I'm sorry," Anna muttered.

"Perhaps you haven't noticed that we are rather busy around here today."

"Of. . .of course," Anna stammered. "I was just looking for my father."

"As you can see, he's not here. Now scat."

Anna scurried out of the room and back to the lobby. Her heart pounded as she sank into the chair next to Richard.

Richard started chuckling. "Something tells me you've been doing something you shouldn't have been doing."

Anna was not amused. "I was just looking for Papa."

"He said to wait here."

"That was a long time ago. Why isn't he finished?"

"A lot of people were hurt in the riot," Richard said. "Papa is a doctor. He has to take care of them."

"But what about Mama and Esther?" Anna asked. "Papa was going to look for them."

"They haven't shown up here," Richard said. "That probably means they are all right."

"How can you be so sure?"

"I'm not sure. But it makes sense."

"I'm getting hungry," Anna said. "We were supposed to eat hours ago. I didn't eat any breakfast because I wanted to be sure I had room for pie."

"I'm sorry about your pie," Richard said softly.

"Right now I would settle for burned toast."

"Me, too."

Anna stood up again.

"Sit down, Anna," Richard said. "Just relax. There's nothing you can do but wait."

"I can't. I'm tired of sitting. I'm tired of this room. I'm tired of this day!"

"It has been a long day," Richard agreed.

Anna started pacing. The crowd in the lobby was thinning

out. People with minor injuries were being released, and their families took them home. Anna stood and looked out the window on the side of the building. The street looked better, she thought. Not so many people were roaming around. As the afternoon gave way to evening, people took shelter in their homes.

Suddenly, Anna lurched forward. She had been pushed from behind. Remembering the feeling of being pushed in the middle of the mob earlier in the day, she panicked for a second. Then she spun around. As she did, Esther grabbed her around the waist.

"Esther! You're all right!" Anna exclaimed. "Where's Mama?"

"Right here," came Mama's voice.

Anna threw herself into her mother's embrace. By now Richard had discovered the arrival of his mother and sister and joined the reunion.

"I'll go find Papa," Richard offered. Off he went, before Anna could tell him not to bother looking in the examination room behind the lobby.

In almost no time, Richard was back with Papa. Anna smiled, relieved, as her parents embraced and then Papa gave Esther a messy kiss on the forehead.

"Over here," Papa said, and he herded his family to an empty corner of the lobby. "I'm so glad you're all right. But where have you been?"

"I didn't know what to think when I lost track of Richard and Anna," Mama said. "I had to trust that the Lord would take care of them. It was all I could do to keep track of Esther in that mob."

"Papa, there were millions and millions of people," Esther said.

Mama smiled. "Thousands at least. I've never seen such a mob, even on a parade day."

"So where did you go?" Anna wanted to know.

"We stayed to the edge of the crowd as much as we could," Mama answered. "I tried to look for you at the next corner from where I lost you. But there were too many people! And they were doing crazy things!"

"We went shopping," Esther blurted out.

"Shopping?" Anna was confused.

"Not exactly," Mama said, "but we saw Mr. Johanssen in the crowd, and he opened up his shop for us. He kept going on to find any women and children who needed help."

"That's a relief," Papa said. "Remind me never to charge him for medical care again!"

"We saw women and children in the street," Richard said. "But some of them were helping with the riot."

"I know," Mama said sadly. "Some of the children didn't understand what was going on. They either got scared or they got excited and joined in."

"Mama," Anna said, "I never found Mr. Olsson. If all the trouble is over, maybe I could go see if he's all right."

"Anna, you are sweet and thoughtful to want to do that," Mama said, "but we can't be sure the streets are safe yet."

"Richard could go with me."

Mama shook her head. "We'll have to find out about Mr. Olsson another way."

"This is the nearest hospital," Richard said. "If he didn't come here, he's probably not hurt."

"He wouldn't come here," Anna said, "because he doesn't have any money to pay doctors."

"If he were seriously hurt," Papa said, "someone would have brought him here anyway."

"I'm hungry," Esther complained. "When are we going to have Easter dinner?"

Mama and Papa looked at each other.

"It looks like we'll have to skip Easter dinner with the family this year," Mama said. "But we can have a simple meal with our own family."

"What will we eat?"

"Let's see what we have."

"I dropped the cherry pie," Anna said sadly. "I hung on to it as long as I could."

"I'm sure you did," Mama said.

"And they were throwing the potatoes in the crowd," Richard said.

"That's all right," Mama answered, "the potatoes were not cooked anyway."

"Then what do we have?" Anna asked.

"I have biscuits!" Esther proclaimed. "They're a little squashed, but I still have them."

"And I've got corn pudding," Mama said, "and apple pie. I'm sorry it's not the pie you made, Anna, but it is a pie."

"Can we eat now?" Esther said. "I'm too hungry to wait until we get home."

Mama and Papa looked at each other again. It was well past suppertime. No one had eaten since before church that morning.

"Certainly," Papa said. "I'm sure I can find some of the trays they use to feed the patients."

While Papa went to find the trays, Mama pulled a little table out of the corner of the room and set the food on it. The bread really was squashed. Anna figured Esther must have been holding it tightly when she was frightened. Anna did not blame her little sister for squashing the bread.

When Papa returned, they gathered around the little table on their knees.

"It's not much of an Easter dinner," Papa said, "but we have a lot to give thanks for."

They held hands as Papa prayed. "Lord, we are grateful

that You have protected our family during the danger today. Thank You for bringing us safely back together. And on this Easter Sunday, we give thanks for the power of the resurrection, when Jesus Christ was raised from the dead so that we could have peace with God. May You grant peace to our city tonight. Amen."

Mama started tearing the bread into chunks. Papa had brought forks for the corn pudding and apple pie.

"Dr. Allerton," called the nurse from the desk, "they need you in the back again."

Papa sighed. "Go ahead and eat. I'll be back as soon as I can."

Anna watched reluctantly as Papa disappeared once again.

CHAPTER 12

A Union Coach

The next baseball practice, on the Tuesday after the riot, did not start out very well. The players straggled to the field late; some of them never arrived at all. Zach came. But no matter how many questions the others asked, he would not explain why he had not played in the game against the Seventh Street Spades.

Richard was just glad Zachary was back. After losing 14 to 2 to the Spades, even Jack Hammond was ready to admit how much they needed Zach's hurling.

After the riot on Easter Sunday, Richard was not sure that either Jack or Zachary would come back to the team. Jack's father had been quoted in the newspaper supporting the union. He criticized people like Kjersten's father—people who had taken jobs away from union members.

Richard hoped that no one would bring up what had happened on Sunday. He would be happy if they could just play ball. Something definitely was wrong with this practice. The Spitfires did not have much fire. They had been practicing hitting fly balls for nearly twenty minutes. No one seemed to have much enthusiasm for the task. Most of the fly balls were actually ground balls. The few balls that did make it into the air fell to the ground. No one seemed to be moving very quickly.

Richard thought that a short game might help. Some competition might light a fire under their feet.

"Let's divide into two squads for a practice game today," Richard suggested. "Tommy, Jack, Elton, and Leland can play against Zach, Tony, Louis, and me," Richard said.

"We'll take the field first," Zach said.

"Fine with me," responded Jack, who headed for home plate.

The teams took their positions. Usually Richard played second base, but with a practice squad of four players, everyone had to cover a lot of territory. He left Tony Tubiera in the infield and trotted out to left field.

Elton came to strike first. He was a good hitter. Richard got ready to chase a long fly ball. Zach lobbed a pitch over home plate. It was not a very good pitch. Elton should have been able to hit it, Richard thought. But Elton did not even try. He just tossed the ball back to Zach on the pitcher's mound.

The next pitch was the same. Before long, Zach had thrown six pitches. Elton had only swung at three of them, and he had hit all of those into foul territory.

Richard shuffled in the outfield. Somehow, he did not think that organizing a practice game was helping anything. Finally,

Elton missed a pitch and struck out.

Tommy came up to bat next. He swung at the first pitch, but not very hard. It dribbled out to Zach, who tossed it to Tony on first base. Tommy did not even try to run to first base.

Watching from the outfield, Richard sighed. Maybe they should just call off the practice, he thought. It certainly seemed as if no one really wanted to play. Richard had not stopped thinking about the riot for two whole days. His parents had discussed it for hours—and then discussed it some more. The teacher had talked about it during school. The other boys were probably thinking about it as much as Richard was. How could they concentrate on baseball?

Elton had not said much yet about the strike or the riot. But Elton usually did not say much. Richard doubted that Elton ever had an idea of his own. If he was asked what he thought about something, he would repeat an opinion he had heard someone else express. Most often, he waited to hear what Tommy Landers thought. Then Elton would act like he had thought of his ideas all on his own. He did not fool anyone but himself.

Tommy, on the other hand, always had an opinion. Sometimes Richard wished Tommy would not talk as much as he did. No matter what the subject was, Tommy had something to say. He could nearly persuade people that the Mississippi River flowed east to west instead of north to south. He knew more facts and figures than anyone else on the team. So if Tommy had an opinion, everyone knew what it was.

Tony was the opposite of Tommy. Richard knew that Tony was smart. He did well in school and could figure out a solution to almost any problem he ran into. Richard knew that Tony had opinions of his own. But Tony never said what he thought. He would just sit in the back of the classroom or stand on the edge of the field and let Tommy do all the talking.

Just then, Leland came up to bat. Richard was tempted to sit down. Leland was a good fielder, but he was not much of a threat with a bat. Nothing much was going to happen now. Leland was always ready for a fight, though. When he came to school on Monday morning, Richard had noticed a strange bruise on the side of Leland's face. He could not help but wonder if Leland had been downtown on Easter Sunday. His father owned a small pottery shop on Bridge Square. Richard did not know what Leland's father thought about the strike. He did not even know what Leland thought about the strike, just that Leland would be ready for a fight on any subject.

Richard was surprised that Henry had shown up at the Tuesday practice. Henry was a nervous boy. If he could concentrate on baseball, he could play fairly well. But he had so much trouble concentrating that he usually bumbled around the field like a five year old. He was always worried about something. He fretted about his homework, he fussed about getting his shoes muddy on rainy days, he muttered about being late for supper. Richard could not imagine how Henry would not be nervous about the streetcar strike, especially after the Easter riot.

And then there were Zach and Jack. They had both shown up at practice, but they had not spoken to each other. Richard did not expect that they would. So far today, no one had mentioned the strike. But how long could that last? Richard wondered. It was on everyone's minds. Sooner or later, someone would bring it up. If Tommy started talking about it and Elton joined in, Zach and Jack would start arguing, and Leland would get in the middle of things just because he wanted to.

Leland struck out, which was exactly what Richard had expected him to do. It was time to change sides.

Richard shuffled in from left field, thinking. He was relieved that Zach had gotten three batters out before Jack had a turn to come to the plate. A contest between Jack and Zach could so easily turn into a fight.

The team needed something to focus on, Richard thought—something besides the strike that everyone in Minneapolis was focused on. If the team did not get their spark back soon, they might never win another game. They would lose to the Oak Lake team in just a few days. All their hard work up until now would be wasted.

Suddenly Richard had just the right idea. He trotted toward the infield and signaled that the whole team should huddle together. Tossing a ball from one hand to the other, Richard shared his idea.

"We've been playing together since we were nine," he said, "and we do pretty well."

"That's right!" exclaimed Tommy. "We're the best."

"The best," echoed Elton.

"But I think we could be better, don't you?" Richard challenged his team.

Heads started bobbing.

"I know just what we need," Richard said. "We need someone with experience to work with us, to teach us, to help us figure out some good plays."

"Are you talking about a coach?" Tony asked.

"That's right," Richard answered excitedly. "We could get our own coach. Some of the other teams are starting to do that."

"I heard that the Oak Lake team has a coach," Elton said.

"Why can't we have a coach, too?" Richard asked. "What do you think, Tony?"

Tony shrugged. "We're doing all right on our own, but we could probably do better with a coach."

"That's exactly what I was thinking," Richard said.

Zachary was starting to warm up to the idea. "We could find someone older than we are—but not too old."

"It has to be someone who really loves baseball," Tommy said. "When you're trying to win a game, attitude counts more than anything else. You can have all the skill in the world, but if your attitude is not right, you'll get nowhere."

Inwardly, Richard agreed. That was exactly the problem the team had.

"Do you really think a coach could help us?" Jack asked.

"Sure!" Richard responded. "We'll find someone who knows how to throw pitches that are hard to hit, someone who can help us with our swings."

"Someone who can hit long fly balls for us to practice catching," Tommy added.

"Exactly!"

"But where would we find someone like that?" Zachary asked. "Who is going to have time to help a boys' team?"

"I think I know someone who would do it," Richard said. He held his breath, getting ready to speak the name he had in mind.

"Who?" Zach asked.

"Yeah, who?" Jack wondered.

"Abe Stevenson."

"Who's Abe Stevenson?" Elton asked.

"I know who that is," erupted Zachary. "That's your cousin."

"He's my second cousin, actually," Richard clarified. "He loves baseball, and he's really good at it."

"Has he ever been a baseball coach before?" Tommy asked. "We need someone with experience, lots of it."

"I don't think he's ever been a coach," Richard said, "but he goes to professional games all the time. He understands the strategies they use. He could teach them to us."

"And you really think he would do it?" Jack was still skeptical.

"I think all we have to do is ask him."

"Wait a minute," Zachary said. "How old is Abe Stevenson?"

"He's eighteen."

"Does he go to college?"

"He's going to go in the fall," Richard said. "He's going to be a scientist."

Zachary was still skeptical. "What does he do now?"

Richard took a deep breath and gave the answer he had hoped to avoid. "He has a temporary job at the railroad station."

"So he's a union man," Zach said flatly.

Richard remembered the day he had seen Abe passing out union leaflets. "The important thing is that Abe understands baseball," Richard insisted.

"Attitude is everything," Tommy said. "We don't need someone coming in here and spreading union propaganda."

"Who said anything about the unions?" Richard countered. "We're talking about a baseball coach. Abe would be perfect."

"Well," Zach said hesitantly as he leaned on a bat. "You did say his job at the railroad was just temporary. He probably hasn't joined the union himself."

"So what if he has joined the union?" Jack snapped.

"We have to be careful who we have around here," Zach said.

"What is that supposed to mean?" Jack pressed.

"Yeah, what is that supposed to mean?" Leland was eager for Zach and Jack to go nose to nose.

"Take it easy," Richard said. "We're talking about baseball, remember?"

"Doesn't Abe's father work at a bank?" Zachary asked.

"Yes, that's right," Richard said.

"So he doesn't come from a union family."

"That's not what matters. We need a coach, and he can help us."

Elton was watching Tommy carefully. Tony shuffled around

the edge of the circle acting like he was not interested in the discussion. Leland's eyes were bright with the hope of an argument. Henry was so nervous his chin twitched.

"I say we give it a try," Tommy said finally.

"Me, too," Elton immediately added.

"I don't suppose it could hurt," Jack conceded.

Richard looked at Zachary. Zach was working his jaw back and forth while he thought about the question. Richard nervously squeezed the ball in his hand.

"All right, we'll give it a try," Zach finally said. "But the minute there is any talk about union nonsense, he leaves the team. Agreed?"

"Agreed." Richard nodded. It was a fair compromise.

CHAPTER 13

A Special Supper

"I hope Kjersten likes chicken," Anna said as she turned over a chicken leg in the simmering lard.

"I'm sure she will like anything that you cook," Mama said. She glanced over Anna's shoulder at the frying chicken.

"I tried to ask her what she likes," Anna continued, "but she didn't understand. The other girls were laughing at me when I was squawking like a chicken."

Mama chuckled. "It probably was funny."

"Kjersten still did not understand. So I don't know if she eats chicken. I don't know anything about what Swedish people eat."

"What does she bring for her lunch at school?" Mama whacked the ends off a bunch of carrots.

"She usually just brings bread. Sometimes she has a piece of fruit."

"Then I'm sure she'll enjoy your biscuits and apple pie."

The biscuits were already out of the oven and wrapped in a cloth to keep them warm until dinner.

"Kjersten's mother makes the most beautiful bread. It's not just a loaf or biscuits. She twists the dough into braids, and the crusts look shiny."

"She probably brushes the top with an egg mixture," Mama said, "to make it shiny."

"I want her to teach me how to make Swedish bread."

"Why don't you ask her?"

"I will—as soon as I learn enough Swedish or Kjersten learns enough English to translate."

"That won't be long," Mama said, "considering how much time you spend with her working on English."

"I'll be so glad when she learns enough English to really talk," Anna said. "On the day after the riot, I tried to ask her if her father was all right. But she didn't understand. It was so frustrating!"

"I'm sure it was frustrating for Kjersten, too," Mama said. "But at least you found out that it was not Mr. Olsson driving that streetcar on Sunday."

"I was so relieved. He was home safe. It was someone who looked like him."

Mama glanced at the perfectly formed pie on the counter next to her daughter. Anna followed her mother's eye.

"Is it time to put the pie in the oven?" Anna asked. She turned over another piece of chicken. The hot lard sizzled and splattered.

"Yes, put the pie in," Mama said. "That way it will be fresh and warm at just the right time."

Anna opened the oven, which was still warm from the biscuits, and set the apple pie in the middle.

"Don't forget to watch the time," Mama said. She tossed

the carrots she had chopped into a pot of boiling water. "Tina and Alison were disappointed that they didn't get to taste your pie on Easter."

"Me, too!" Anna said. "It was my first pie, and it was perfect, but no one got to take even a bite."

"I'm sure this one will not go to waste."

"Mama, are we going to have another family dinner?" Anna asked. "Can we make up for missing Easter dinner?"

"Alison has suggested that," Mama said. "We all want to do it."

"Even Uncle Enoch and Uncle Charles?"

Mama sighed. "Enoch and Charles have finally found something to agree on. They have different opinions about the strike, but they both think that turning over a streetcar and starting a riot was not necessary."

"Does that mean they're ready to be friends again?"

"It might be a first step."

Someone knocked on the front door.

"Kjersten!" Anna cried. She snatched up a towel and tried to rub the grease off her hands.

By the time Anna got to the front door, Esther already had it open. Kjersten looked relieved to see Anna.

"This is my sister, Esther," Anna said, taking Kjersten's hand and pulling her into the living room. Kjersten smiled nervously.

"And this is my mother," Anna continued.

Kjersten nodded her head politely. With one hand, she clutched a small bundle close to her chest.

"Esther," Mama said, "run and find Papa and Richard. Tell them our guest is here."

"Come in and sit down," Anna said. She led Kjersten to a chair. "Sit," she said, and she demonstrated by sitting in the chair next to Kjersten. The nervous Swedish girl sat down, still clutching her bundle. Her faded yellow calico dress hung down over her scuffed brown boots. But her eyes were bright with anticipation.

"I'm going to check on the chicken," Mama said.

Anna was tempted to flap her elbows and squawk but decided not to. It was too late to change the menu. Either Kjersten would eat chicken or she would not.

Esther returned with Papa and Richard. Kjersten smiled at Richard, whom she recognized.

"This is my papa," Anna said.

Papa extended his hand. "I am pleased to meet you."

Kjersten put her small white hand in Papa's big hand. "Nice." Now she thrust the small bundle toward Anna.

"What is this?" Anna asked.

"Give," Kjersten said.

"Give? Is it a gift?"

Kjersten nodded. "I give."

Anna laid the bundle in her lap and began unwrapping it. Kjersten's family was very poor. What kind of gift could she have brought?

Anna gasped in delight when the package lay open in her lap.

"Dolls!" Esther squealed.

Three small painted wooden dolls lay in Anna's lap. They were only a few inches tall, but they were painted with exquisite detail in bright colors and a glossy finish.

"These are beautiful!" Anna exclaimed. "Look, Mama," she said as her mother came back into the room, "look what Kjersten brought."

Mama picked up one of the dolls. "Look at that little face," she said. "Why, Anna, it almost looks like you."

Anna turned to her friend. "Kjersten, where did you get these?"

Kjersten did not understand.

"Buy?" Anna said. "Store?"

Kjersten shook her head. "No. No store. I make."

"You made these?" Somehow the dolls seemed even more beautiful now.

Kjersten gestured as if she were holding a carving knife. "Papa."

"Your papa carves the dolls?"

Now she moved her fingers delicately as if she were painting. "Kjersten."

"Your papa carves the dolls, and you paint them."

Kjersten nodded vigorously.

"They are a beautiful gift," Anna said. "Thank you."

"I think supper is just about ready," Mama said.

"Great!" Richard said. "I'm famished."

Anna showed Kjersten the way to the kitchen. They all sat down around the table. Kjersten bowed her head along with all the Allertons, and Papa gave thanks for the food and for Anna's new friend.

Mama had put the chicken on a platter, and she started passing it around the table. The boiled carrots followed, along with a bowl of mashed potatoes.

"Where are the biscuits?" Esther asked.

"We almost forgot." Anna popped over to the sideboard and fetched the basket of biscuits.

Esther took two biscuits and passed the basket to Richard.

Anna watched Kjersten carefully as she took a small portion of everything that was passed. When the platter of chicken came to Kjersten, she started giggling.

"What's so funny?" Anna asked.

Kjersten covered her mouth in embarrassment. But she could not stop giggling. Soon she flapped her elbows in the air and squawked.

The whole Allerton family burst out laughing.

"Yes," Anna said, flapping her elbows, too. "Chicken."

"I think she understands now," Mama said, smiling.

"Chicken," repeated Anna.

"Shikeen," said Kjersten.

"Chicken. Do you like chicken?" Anna asked.

Kjersten picked up the chicken leg on her plate and took a big bite. Anna leaned back in her chair, relieved. Everyone ate contentedly.

"The chicken is delicious," Papa said. He helped himself to a second piece.

"Thank you," Anna responded. She glanced at Kjersten, and they almost started giggling again.

After awhile, Mama said, "Don't forget to check the pie."

Anna scooted her chair back and crossed the kitchen to the oven. Peeking in, she said, "I think it's done."

Protecting her hands with two folded dish towels, Anna removed the pie from the hot oven and set it on the sideboard.

"It looks perfect!" Mama said proudly. The crust had baked to a golden brown. Steam rose through the holes Anna had pricked in the top of the pie.

Esther pushed her plate away. "I'm ready for pie."

Mama inspected Esther's plate. She had eaten all of her supper. "All right," Mama said, "but don't take more pie than you can eat."

Anna took a stack of plates down from a shelf and started serving the pie. Mama cleared the dinner plates from the table.

Anna set a slice of pie in front of her little sister and another in front of her brother. "You two have the privilege of being the first tasters," she said.

Esther stuck her fork in the pie and shoveled a piece into her mouth. Richard did the same.

As Anna brought plates to the table for Kjersten and her father, she saw Esther spitting out her first bite of pie.

"Esther!" Mama scolded.

"I'm sorry, Mama, but it doesn't taste like your apple pie."

"She's right," Richard said. His face was contorted and his cheeks puffed out as he tried not to spit out the bite of pie. With a great effort, he forced it down his throat. "This doesn't taste like anyone's apple pie."

Anna's heart started pounding. What was wrong with her perfect pie?

Papa gingerly took the tiniest piece of pie on the end of his fork and put it to his lips. Even before he put it in his mouth, he knew what was wrong. He started laughing.

"Anna, how much sugar did you put in this?" Papa asked.

"One cup, just like the recipe called for."

"And where did you get the sugar from?"

Anna whirled around to look at the canisters on the counter. Then she groaned. "I used salt!"

"A whole cup of salt!" Richard said. He put his fork down, grimacing.

Anna snatched away the plate she had just set in front of Kjersten. Her friend was confused.

"No good," Anna said. "No good."

"Kjersten like pie," her friend said.

Anna shook her head hard. "Not this pie. This pie is bad." She made a sour face. Anna nudged the platter of chicken toward Kjersten. "Have some more chicken."

Kjersten started giggling all over again. Esther and Richard flapped their arms. Mama and Papa roared.

The kitchen full of human chickens almost made Anna forget about her disastrous pie.

Mama took the plates from Richard and Esther, laughing. "Anna, you go visit with your friend. Papa can help me clean up tonight."

In the living room, Anna pouted for a few minutes. She dropped her first pie in the Easter riot. Now she'd put salt in the next one. Would she ever make a pie that anyone could eat?

105

She pushed her straggling blond hair away from her face.

Kjersten's hair was neatly tied in tight braids. Anna's hung loose round her shoulders, with two floppy bows on top of her head. She touched the end of one of Kjersten's braids.

"This is pretty," she said.

Kjersten reached out and took hold of Anna's hair. With skilled fingers, she started braiding.

"Can you braid my hair?" Anna asked.

Kjersten's finger's kept moving.

"Wait," Anna said, "I want you to do all of it." She pulled a straight back chair away from the wall and sat in it. Kjersten combed her fingers through Anna's hair, making it do exactly what she wanted it to do. After she had made two tight, neat braids, she moved the bows from the top of Anna's head to the bottom of the braids. Finally, she stood back, satisfied with her work.

Anna got up and stood in front of the brass-rimmed looking glass next to the front door. Kjersten stood next to her. They smiled at their matching blond braids and blue eyes.

"You two could be sisters!" Richard had come into the room and looked at their reflection in the glass. "Anna, you really look Swedish!"

Anna smiled. "I think it would be fun to go to another country. Maybe someday I'll go to Sweden."

Kjersten stepped away from the mirror and peered out at the darkness beyond the front door. "I go," she said quietly.

"Already!" Anna moaned.

"Papa said he would walk Kjersten home," Richard said. "She shouldn't go by herself now that it's dark."

After Papa and Kjersten were gone, Mama said, "Your friend is very nice, Anna. And you're doing a wonderful job teaching her English. She understands quite a bit."

"At least now she knows what 'chicken' means! I don't understand how anyone could not like Kjersten."

CHAPTER 14

Kjersten's Gift

When Anna went to school the next morning, she still wore her hair in braids. She liked the braids, and she did not mind one bit if she looked Swedish.

"People are going to get you confused with Kjersten," Richard had told her.

Anna had simply tossed her braids over her shoulders and said, "I don't care."

They got to school early. The bell would not ring for almost twenty minutes. Esther scampered off to play with girls her own age.

"I'm going to go find some of the boys from the team," Richard said, "and let them know Abe is coming to practice tomorrow."

Anna scanned the schoolyard for Kjersten, but she was not there yet. Shifting her bundle of books to the other shoulder, Anna started over to the corner of the schoolyard where Kjersten liked to sit. She would wait for her friend there.

She nearly ran into Martha Wilkerson.

"Anna Allerton, what have you done to yourself?" Martha said, laughing loudly.

"What do you mean?" Anna responded, even though she knew what Martha was talking about.

"Your hair! It's in braids!"

"So? Haven't you ever seen braids before?"

"Of course I have—just not on you."

"I never tried them before, but I like them."

"You look like you just got off the boat from Sweden."

Martha had dark hair and dark eyes. No one would ever mistake her for a Swedish immigrant. Like Anna's family, the Wilkersons had been in America for generations.

"We all have to come from somewhere," Anna said.

"Why do you want to be Swedish? What's wrong with being American?"

"What's wrong with being Swedish?" Anna countered.

"Anna, why are you so crazy lately? I never see you anymore. You always eat lunch with that new girl."

"Her name is Kjersten," Anna said. "And there's plenty of room on the bench for you to sit with us."

"Now you're acting just like her, even fixing your hair the way she does. Are you going to stop speaking English?"

Anna lifted her chin. *"Tack sa mycket."*

"Stop it, Anna!"

"Martha, Swedish is just another language. Kjersten is just

108

like you and me and all the other girls. She's smart and funny and works hard. When she learns more English, you'll find out for yourself."

Martha looked doubtful. "We've all known each other all our lives. I have enough friends already."

"But Kjersten doesn't," Anna said. "What if your father decided to move your family to Europe and you had to leave all your friends?"

Martha was not sure what to say. "My father wouldn't do that," she muttered.

"There's Kjersten now," Anna said, seeing Kjersten come through the gate. "Let's go talk to her."

"Um, you go," Martha said. "I see Samantha coming in at the other gate, and I need to talk to her."

Martha hurried off to Samantha and her familiar cluster of friends. Shaking her head, Anna crossed the yard to greet Kjersten.

At the same moment, they put their elbows in the air and flapped and squawked.

"Chicken good," Kjersten said.

"I'm glad you liked it."

Kjersten smiled. "Pie not good."

"Shhh. Don't tell anyone about that."

Behind them, Martha snickered. Anna glared at Martha. Apparently talking to Martha had done no good at all. Samantha, however, had stopped snickering. Anna saw her looking at Kjersten as if she was really interested in her.

They moved to a bench and put their books down. Anna reached into the roomy pocket of her skirt and pulled out two of the dolls Kjersten had given her the night before. She set them on the bench.

"These are beautiful," Anna said. "I couldn't stand to leave them home."

Two other girls had joined Martha and Samantha. Martha was pointing at Anna and Kjersten.

Anna had an idea. She took hold of the dolls and held them up in the air. Loudly, she said, "You did such a beautiful job painting these dolls. I hope that you will teach me how to do it."

She turned the dolls in several directions. Their bright colors gleamed in the sunlight.

Kjersten was puzzled.

Anna pointed to Kjersten and then herself. "You," she said slowly, "teach me." And she held her fingers together as if she were holding a paintbrush. She glanced at the other girls. They were watching.

"Painting the dolls is very difficult," Anna said loudly. "You have a special talent. Not everyone could do such beautiful work."

Anna knew she was talking too much and Kjersten was not understanding. But Martha and Samantha and the others understood. She had their attention now. In a group, they were slowly walking toward the bench where Kjersten and Anna sat. Anna watched them out of the side of her eye while she continued to talk to Kjersten. When the four girls were close enough to cast a shadow on Kjersten, Anna turned to speak directly to them.

"Would you like to see my new dolls?" Anna said to the girls. "Kjersten gave them to me. She painted them herself."

Unsure, the other girls looked at each other. Finally Martha nodded her head. "Okay. We'll look at them."

They gathered around the bench. Anna passed around the two dolls.

"I've never seen anything like this," Samantha said. "Did she really paint them herself?"

"Of course she did," Anna said. "She brought three of them to my house last night, all different sizes."

"Where does she get the dolls?"

"Her father carves them."

Martha's eyes widened in interest. "Her father carves the dolls, and she paints them?"

Anna nodded.

Martha looked at Kjersten, then asked Anna, "Does she understand what we're saying?"

"Slow down, and use short words," Anna suggested.

"Are you sure?"

"Go ahead," Anna urged.

Martha turned to Kjersten. "Very pretty," she said, holding one of the dolls.

"Dank you," Kjersten said, smiling.

Anna smiled, too. The beautiful dolls were a language of their own. Girls from across the ocean could enjoy the same beauty.

Across the schoolyard, Richard was trying to stay out of an argument. He had joined the group of boys, hoping to talk about baseball. But they were more interested in the strike.

Tommy, as usual, was not afraid to say what he was thinking. "It was crazy to turn over a streetcar. The people who did that should be arrested and locked up."

"All ten thousand of them?" someone asked.

"There were ten thousand people at the riot," Tommy said, "but not all of them turned over the streetcars. Only a few did that."

Richard could still picture the faces of the men who had rocked the streetcar till it toppled.

"Tommy, I thought your father was in the union," Leland said. "Why are you siding with the streetcar company?"

"I'm not siding with anybody," Tommy said. "I'm just saying they didn't have to turn over two streetcars."

"They had to do something to get the attention of Thomas

Lowry. My father says that Lowry won't even talk to the union leaders."

Tommy made a face. "Do you really think that destroying a streetcar is going to make Lowry give the drivers back their wages? Lowry is not the kind of person to be frightened by something like that. In fact, it's likely to make him even angrier."

Richard thought Tommy had a good point.

Jack Hammond could not hold his feelings in any longer. "If Lowry can do whatever he wants to do with the drivers' pay, then the drivers can do whatever they want with the streetcars."

Zachary gritted his teeth. "Cutting the drivers' pay was a business decision. Lowry wasn't trying to hurt anybody."

"Maybe he didn't try to hurt anybody," Jack said, "but he did. All he cares about is making himself richer."

"It's his business. He has a right to make a profit."

Jack's face was flaming red. "Does he have a right to take food away from my little sisters?"

"He didn't do that."

"Yes, he did!"

"No, he didn't."

Zachary swung at Jack, who ducked just in time.

"Get 'em!" cried Leland, always ready for a fight.

"Stop!" Henry shouted. "Please don't hurt each other. Please stop!"

Jack's right fist connected with Zach's left eye.

"Jack Hammond, stop this nonsense," Richard yelled. He grabbed Jack's arm and twisted it behind his back.

"He started it," Zach said, glaring at Jack.

"No, I didn't."

"Yes, you did."

The bell rang just then. All across the schoolyard, students started shuffling their way into the building.

Inside the classroom, Richard took his usual seat behind

Jack and across from Zachary. Jack and Zach glared at each other. Zach's eye was swelling up and had turned an angry red.

"We're not finished," Zach muttered, scowling at Jack.

Jack scoffed. "Just remember who punched you."

A shadow crossed Richard's desk. Miss Wickham, the teacher, stood in the aisle between Zach and Jack.

"I understand there was a dispute in the schoolyard this morning," she said.

Jack and Zach stared straight ahead. Neither of them said anything.

"It is my understanding that this dispute centered on the reasonableness of the riot last Sunday. Is that correct?"

Again, no one spoke. Miss Wickham began pacing the aisle.

"Mr. Allerton," the teacher said, "I believe you were present during the riot. Is that correct?"

"Yes, ma'am."

"Were you participating?"

"No, ma'am! I was on my way to Easter dinner and got trapped."

"So I understand. Perhaps you would like to comment for the class on what you saw."

Richard gulped and awkwardly stood next to his desk. "People were angry," he said softly. "They were saying mean things about each other—about their own neighbors. A few weeks ago it didn't matter that one friend was a manager at the mill and another friend drove a streetcar. But now, people are choosing their friends based on how they earn a living."

"And do you find this reasonable?" Miss Wickham asked.

Richard shook his head. "No, ma'am. It's not fair." Richard looked at Zach and Jack. "A friend is a friend, no matter what."

Jack turned around in his seat and looked at Richard. "But what if the friend you trusted does something to hurt you? Is he still a friend?"

Richard thought for a moment. "I think that it is not always easy to understand why a person does something. And until we understand, we shouldn't get all riled up."

"Thank you, Mr. Allerton," the teacher said. "That is a very reasonable opinion."

Relieved, Richard sat down.

"And now, if you will please turn your attention to the task at hand," Miss Wickham droned, "we will begin our day with the mathematics assignment."

Richard opened his notebook. Zachary and Jack did the same. They still did not look at each other. Had they listened to anything that was said? Richard wondered.

CHAPTER 15

The Tense Practice

"This is a terrific idea, Richard." Abe Stevenson strode down the street next to his young cousin with a bat propped over his shoulder. At eighteen and a half, Abe was tall, with lanky legs and a long stride. His dark hair often looked like it needed to be combed. Richard had enjoyed being with Abe for as long as he could remember.

"I promised the team you would say yes," Richard said, "so I'm sure glad you did."

"How could I say no to coaching a baseball team?"

"I thought you might be too busy. You have a job, and I know that you're really a scientist."

"I'm glad you recognize that, Richard, because I think it's about time I started teaching you about science as well as baseball."

"Do you mean that?" Richard said excitedly. "Can we work in your lab together?"

"Absolutely. But there's always time for baseball. You have a sharp team. I've seen you play. So I know this will be fun."

Richard sighed heavily. "The last game was a disaster. I'm glad you weren't there. It was so embarrassing."

Abe chuckled. "I heard about it. It seems you lost your hurler. Has he come back to the team?"

"He was at practice on Tuesday, but I don't know if he'll come back today." Richard winced at the memory of Jack's fist hitting Zach's eye.

They turned a corner to head in the direction of the baseball field.

"I know you can help us," Richard said. "But I have to warn you. Not everyone may want your help."

"Every coach has to win over some players—even on professional teams." Abe moved the bat to the other shoulder. "A good coach has to prove himself. I know I have to show that I understand baseball from the inside out."

If only it were that simple, Richard thought. *If only the boys on the team would think about baseball and not unions and strikes.*

"You seem a little nervous," Abe said.

Richard shrugged. "Getting a coach was my idea. Asking you was my idea. If—"

"If this doesn't work out, you'll look bad to the boys on your team." Abe finished Richard's thought. "Don't worry, Richard. I can make this work."

"How?"

"I'll just approach it scientifically. I'll make a hypothesis about what I think will happen, then I'll try some ideas to see if the hypothesis is true."

Richard chuckled and felt more at ease.

They arrived at the practice field. Most of the boys were there already. Richard got their attention and signaled that they should gather around home plate.

"This is Abe Stevenson, our new coach," Richard said proudly.

"Hello, boys," Abe said brightly.

"This is Jack. He plays first base," Richard said, beginning the introductions. "And this is Tommy and Tony and Elton and Louis, Leland, and Henry." Richard scanned the field. "I don't see Zachary. He's the hurler."

"He's probably not coming," Tony said.

"He's just late," said Henry.

"No, he's not coming," Tony insisted.

Abe jumped in. "Let's give him a few minutes more. In the meantime, why don't we get started?"

"Just a minute." Tommy was leaning on a bat with a suspicious expression on his face. "I have a few questions to ask the new coach."

"Sure," Abe said. "Ask anything you'd like."

"Have you ever coached a baseball team before?"

"No, but I've played baseball all my life. I taught Richard everything he knows."

That seemed to impress Tommy. Richard was a good player.

"What position did you play?" Tommy continued his inquisition.

"Most of the time I played in the outfield. I have a pretty good arm for throwing the ball back into the infield."

"Can you hit?"

"Better than average," Abe said confidently. "I can get a hit when I really need one."

"How many professional games have you seen?"

"Oh, dozens, maybe hundreds," Abe answered. "I go whenever I can with my uncle Charles."

"He's a railroad man, isn't he?" Tony asked.

"Yes, he is."

"Is he in the union?"

Richard's stomach tightened. But Abe was not flustered. "Hey, are we here to talk politics or to play ball?"

"Play ball!" exclaimed Leland.

"Then let's get to it." Abe clapped his hands several times. "You're going to have to show me what you can do today. Then we can work out some plays."

"What do you want us to do?" Richard asked.

"Set up a batting practice rotation," Abe answered. "I want to see your swings."

Richard nodded.

"Jack, go on over to first base," Abe said. "I'll pitch. The rest of you can get in the hitting rotation."

The boys set up their formation. Elton batted first. Abe threw him an easy pitch, but it was a little high. Elton let it pass.

"Good eye, good eye," Abe said.

He threw the next ball. This one was right down the center of the strike zone. Elton swung. The ball bounced through the infield, an easy ground ball.

Abe went and stood behind Elton. "Let's work on that swing for a minute," Abe said. They grasped the bat together. "You have a lot of power, Elton. But your swing is not quite even. You're hitting the top of the ball. That's what makes it become a grounder."

Abe moved the bat to show what he meant.

"Keep your swing even, and you'll get the ball into the air." They swung together again. "It'll take a lot of practice, but you'll get it."

Richard looked around the field. The team seemed to be interested in what Abe had to say. But Zach was still missing. Tony was probably right, Richard thought. Why would Zach come to play baseball after Jack had given him a black eye?

It was Leland's turn to bat. He grasped the bat at the very

bottom and stood poised with his arms over the plate. Abe threw the pitch. Leland swung and hit the ball on the center of the bat. It was a line drive that lost its energy and plopped to the ground at second base.

"Good swing," Abe said, "nice and even. But try stepping back from the plate a little bit. Then you can hit the ball with the end of the bat. It will have a lot more power and go farther."

Abe showed Leland where to stand, then pitched again. This time, Leland swung and belted the ball into right field. The team whooped its encouragement.

In right field, Richard scooped up the ball and threw it back to Abe on the pitcher's mound. Leland had run safely to second base—something that almost never happened to Leland.

When Richard turned to go back to his position in right field, he spotted Zachary leaning against the fence. He started to wave to Zach and to call him over. Then he changed his mind. If Zach wanted to play baseball, all he had to do was join the team.

Jack picked up a bat next. Richard knew that Jack already had a straight, even swing. He wondered what Abe's comment would be.

Jack hit the first pitch. He threw the bat down awkwardly and started to run. The ball went to second base, where Henry snatched it up and threw it to first base. In a real game, Jack would have been out.

"Nice try, Jack," Abe said. "You have a nice swing. Let me just suggest one thing." He picked up a bat to demonstrate. "As you swing, start taking a step with your left foot. After you connect with the ball, let the bat swing around in your left hand and let it go. Don't worry about it. If you lift your foot on the swing, you'll be one step on your way to first base. You might have been able to beat out that throw."

Jack nodded enthusiastically. "I'll try that next time."

The batting practice continued. Tommy and Tony and Henry took their turns. Abe patiently diagnosed the swings of each player.

Out in the field, Richard kept an eye on Zach. The hurler's hands had come out of the pockets of his trousers, and he had moved along the fence closer to the infield—closer to Abe. Richard saw Zach listening carefully to everything Abe said.

"Now I want to see how well you can field," Abe called out to the team members. "I'll hit some fly balls. You try to catch them and throw them back in."

The team spread out around the field. Zach left the fence and joined the practice. He stood deep in left field only a few feet away from the fence. But he had definitely joined the practice. Excited, Richard pretended not to notice. He leaned forward, his hands on his knees, ready for the first fly ball.

Richard stood between Jack in left field and Zach in right field. Both of them concentrated on Abe. Richard did not see any dirty looks going back and forth. They were there to play baseball.

Abe tossed a ball in the air and swung. The ball sailed into left field. Jack scrambled to get under the ball and held his hands high. Judging the arc of the ball carefully, he took a few steps back. The ball plopped into his hands. Grinning, he heaved it back to the infield for Abe to hit again.

"That was pretty good," Tommy called out. "For someone who usually plays first base, you do pretty well in the outfield."

"Thanks!" Jack called back.

Jack drifted toward Richard in center field.

"Your cousin is really good," Jack said to Richard. "I never noticed how I wasn't taking a step with my swing. That's really going to help."

"I've learned a lot from Abe," Richard said.

"You're lucky to have a cousin to teach you," Jack said.

"Jack is right." Zach had drifted over from left field. "You're lucky to have Abe teaching you, and now we're all lucky to have him coaching our team."

Richard watched, holding his breath, as Zachary and Jack started to talk to each other.

"How's your eye?" Jack muttered.

"Not too bad."

"We thought you weren't coming."

"I thought about not coming."

"But you're here."

"This is my team," Zach said. "Where else am I going to go to play?"

Jack shrugged. "The Seventh Street team would be happy to have you."

"Naw. They don't have a coach."

Jack nodded. "You're right. We're the best. We have a coach."

"Even if he's a union man?" Zach asked.

"He's a ballplayer, through and through. That's what matters."

"Heads up!" Richard shouted. Abe had smacked another fly ball to the outfield. He raised his eyes to the sky and tried to follow the path of the ball.

Zachary and Jack were doing the same thing. None of them was watching what the others were doing. The flight of the ball brought them close together. They smacked into each other and tumbled into a heap. The ball dropped to the ground and dribbled past them.

The three boys broke into laughter. Untangling themselves, they got to their feet again.

Jack was rubbing his head. "Whose foot was that?" he asked, laughing.

"I'll probably have two black eyes now," Zach responded.

Richard looked up and saw Abe waving them in. They trotted in to the pitcher's mound.

121

"Let's have a short game, three innings," Abe said. "We'll divide up into two teams."

"I want Zach on my team," Jack said.

"But he's the best hurler," whined Elton. "Who will hurl for our team?"

"That's your problem," Jack snapped, grinning.

"At least let us have Tommy for hitting," Elton said.

"You've got a deal. Let's play ball!"

Richard took up his usual position at second. Zach was on the pitcher's mound, and Jack was over on first base where he belonged. They snapped the ball around the infield.

The spark was back.

CHAPTER 16

A Disappointing Party

The doors opened and the children poured out of the school building into the bright sunshine of an April afternoon. Richard and Anna met each other in their usual spot and looked around for Esther. Anna had promised Mama she would walk Esther home.

"Anna, look!" Esther cried as she ran up to join them. "A streetcar!"

Anna turned to look, and indeed a streetcar was rumbling past. At least ten passengers were riding inside. Now it was Anna's turn to get excited.

"Richard, it's Jack's father. Mr. Hammond is driving the streetcar!"

Richard looked carefully. "You're right. The strike must be over."

Martha Wilkerson was nearby. "The strike definitely is over," she informed them. "The drivers did not get their two cents an hour back. They have to work on Mr. Lowry's terms or not at all." Martha tossed her hair over her shoulder haughtily.

"You don't have to be so excited," Richard said. "A lot of families got hurt during the strike."

"They caused all that trouble for nothing," Martha retorted.

"The important think is that it's over," Anna said. "Everyone can go back to work, and things can go back to normal."

"I want to find Jack and talk to him," Richard said.

"You go ahead," Anna said. "I'm going home. I have to finish getting ready for Kjersten's party."

"Can I come to the party?" Esther pleaded.

"I'm giving a birthday party for Kjersten," Anna said. "It's not for little kids."

"I'm not little, I'm eight."

"You'll have to be on your best behavior."

"I can behave, I promise."

"All right, then, but we have to hurry. I don't want Kjersten to get there before we do." She turned and waived at Martha. "See you at the party, Martha."

Martha did not answer.

Anna and Esther scurried toward home. Richard scanned the schoolyard looking for Jack.

He found Jack huddled with a group of boys, most of them from the baseball team. Even Zach was there.

"I saw your father driving," Richard said. "I know he would never go against the union, so I guess this means the strike is over."

"It's over all right," grumbled Jack. "And Thomas Lowry won."

"I heard that the drivers didn't get the wage cut back."

"That's right. They got nothing. Thomas Lowry got it all, so he can stuff his fat, filthy pockets." Jack did not seem at all relieved that the strike was over.

"At least your father is working again," Richard said.

"And the streetcars are running!" Tommy Landers said excitedly. "I was getting really tired of walking everywhere. I'm going to go downtown right now. I'm going to ride a street-car all the way to Bridge Square and back."

"If you do," Jack said, "you're just putting more money in Thomas Lowry's pockets."

Richard looked at Zach, who had not said a word. He could be gloating, Richard thought. He could be boasting about the victory of Thomas Lowry. But Zachary said nothing.

"Does anyone want to play ball for a few minutes?" Richard asked.

"I do," Zach quickly responded.

Several others joined in, and soon they were playing three against three.

"A birthday pie?" Esther asked, giggling. "I think that's silly!"

"It's what Kjersten wanted," Anna said. "Since she didn't get to eat pie when she came for supper, I promised to make her one for her birthday."

"Are you going to put candles in it?"

"Of course."

Esther giggled again.

Anna ignored Esther and continued her preparations for the party. She had made the pie early in the morning before school, but she had not baked it yet. She wanted it to be fresh and hot from the oven for the party. So she opened the oven and put the pie in.

Then she turned her attention to the dining room. Mama had

agreed to let Anna have the party in the dining room. Kjersten had never had a real birthday party before. Anna wanted this party to be one Kjersten would remember for a long time.

After the girls at school discovered Kjersten's talent with the painted dolls, they seemed to welcome her a little more warmly. Anna did not hear so many of them snickering behind Kjersten's back. Samantha, especially, was intrigued by the dolls and wanted to learn to paint them herself. So Anna had invited Martha and Samantha and Edith and Alice to the party. There would be just enough pie to go around.

Pink was Kjersten's favorite color. Last night, Anna had decorated the dining room with as much pink as she could find, from the tablecloth to paper streamers tied to the lights. A big sign propped up on the buffet said, "Happy Birthday, Kjersten." Her gift for Kjersten was wrapped in pink tissue paper and placed in the center of the table.

A knock sounded at the front door. Esther jumped up. "I'll get it."

Just as Anna thought, Kjersten had arrived.

"I early?" Kjersten asked. Her cheeks were pink.

"Did you run all the way?" Esther asked.

Kjersten nodded.

"You're right on time," Anna answered. "The others will be here soon. Now close your eyes."

Kjersten looked puzzled. Anna put her hands over Kjersten's eyes, making her friend giggle.

She led Kjersten into the dining room. There, she removed her hands. The Swedish girl gasped. "Pretty! For me?"

"Yes, it's for you," Anna said smiling. "Happy birthday, Kjersten."

Kjersten spun around and hugged Anna. "Dank you, dank you, Anna."

Esther nudged her way in between them. "Where are the

other girls?" she asked.

"They're coming," Anna said confidently. "We just got out of school. They probably had to go home and get their gifts for Kjersten."

"Will you braid my hair while you wait?" Esther asked Kjersten.

Anna looked to be sure Kjersten had understood. Kjersten was already separating Esther's hair into the strands that would become twin braids.

The clock in the hall ticked loudly. Anna tried not to look at it too often. The truth was she was not sure if the other girls were coming. Anna watched as Kjersten nimbly braided Esther's hair. Esther was sitting perfectly still. It would not be long at all before the job was done. For once, Anna wished that Esther would wiggle a little bit. But Esther had promised to be on her best behavior, and she was.

The clock ticked.

Finally someone knocked on the door. Anna leaped out of her chair and ran to open the door.

"Samantha! Hello!"

"Hello, Anna," Samantha said. She stood on the front porch awkwardly holding a small package. She wore a sapphire blue satin dress that highlighted her eyes beautifully. Anna had never seen her look so lovely, but she had not expected Samantha to change from her cotton school frock into such a fancy dress.

"Come in." Anna opened the door wide. She glanced over her shoulder at the dining room, grinning. "Where are the others?"

Samantha shuffled into the house. "I'm not sure," she muttered.

Anna was puzzled. "Didn't you talk to Martha today—or Edith or Alice? They were all in school today."

Samantha licked her lips nervously. "I don't think they're coming," she said quietly.

Anna closed the door and leaned against it.

"What do you mean," she asked.

"I asked them all if they were coming," Samantha said, "because I can't stay. I wanted someone to bring my gift."

"You can't stay?" Anna asked.

"My mother says I have to go have dinner at my grandmother's house. My aunt just got engaged, and they're having a party for her tonight. Mama's waiting out in the carriage."

"So that's why you're in your best dress."

"I'm sorry, Anna."

"It's all right, Samantha. You have to do what your mother wants you to do."

"I'm sorry about the others, too."

"That's not your fault," Anna said.

"Here, please give this to Kjersten," Samantha said, placing the small package in Anna's hands.

"Don't you want to say happy birthday to Kjersten yourself?"

"My mother is waiting. We have to go look for my brother Tommy."

"But, Samantha—"

"I'm sorry. I have to go."

Then she was gone. Anna turned back to the dining room. Determined not to let Kjersten see the disappointment she felt, she marched into the room.

"Look what Samantha brought for you," she said brightly.

"Where is Samantha?" Esther asked.

"She couldn't stay," Anna explained. "She had to go to her aunt's engagement party."

"Samantha go?" Kjersten said weakly.

Anna nodded. "She wanted to stay, but she couldn't."

Kjersten did not respond. Her lower lip quivered.

"I think it's time we get this party started," Anna said.

"But no one's here," Esther commented.

Anna shot her sister a pointed look. "We're here," she said emphatically. "We don't need a whole roomful of people in order to have a party."

"They're not coming, are they?" Esther said. "They didn't want to come to Kjersten's party."

Anna wanted to give her sister a good shake and send her out of the room.

"That just means more pie for us," Anna said, grinning.

But Kjersten was not fooled. She had understood enough of what Esther said to know that no one was coming to her birthday party. She sank into a chair. "Girls not come," she said sadly.

Anna said quietly, "No, the other girls are not coming."

Kjersten set Samantha's gift on the table next to Anna's.

"They not like me," she said.

"They don't know you," Anna insisted. "If they would get to know you, they would like you as much as I do."

Kjersten stared at the floor.

"Let's open the gifts," Esther suggested.

"That's a wonderful idea," Anna said. She sat down next to Kjersten and once again put the package from Samantha in her hands.

Slowly, Kjersten unwrapped the box and opened it. Inside lay a neat row of six bright paint colors and two new brushes. Kjersten's face brightened. "New paint! I need!"

"That was a thoughtful gift," Anna said.

"Open Anna's present," Esther urged. From the other side of the table, she nudged the package toward Kjersten.

Kjersten gently removed three layers of pink tissue paper and opened her mouth in delight. "Pretty!" She held up one of twelve colorful ribbons Anna had wrapped up, two each of six different colors.

"I got them from Mr. Johanssen's shop," Anna explained. "I'll have to take you there. But maybe you already know him. He's Swedish, too, after all. He has lovely things in his shop. He might even like to sell your dolls. Your father could carve them, you could paint them, and Mr. Johanssen can sell them." She clapped her hands in delight at her own idea. "I'll talk to him right away."

Kjersten laughed. She had not understood much of Anna's speech. "Anna talk much," she said.

"How is the party going?" Mama had just appeared in the doorway.

Kjersten smiled at Mama. "Presents nice."

"I'm glad you like them."

"Is it time for pie?" Esther asked eagerly.

Anna glanced at the clock. "It should be just about done."

Mama sniffed the air. "It doesn't smell like you're baking a pie."

Anna's stomach sank. Mama was right. By now the house ought to be filled with the aroma of sweetened fruit. She jumped out of her chair and dashed into the kitchen.

Pulling the oven door open, she looked at her pie. It was formed perfectly. But it was still pasty white and raw. She groaned.

"I forgot to ask you to light the oven," she said to Mama. "It should have been baking all this time."

"I'll light the oven now," Mama offered.

"It's too late," Anna said. "Kjersten has to go home soon." Esther and Kjersten came into the kitchen.

"What's wrong with the pie this time?" Esther asked.

Anna's face crumpled.

"The pie is perfect," Mama said, "it's just not baked."

"No pie?" Kjersten asked, confused.

Anna shook her head. "No pie." She opened the oven door

and showed Kjersten. Instantly, Kjersten understood. She started giggling.

"Why are you laughing?" Anna said. "I've ruined your party. We don't have a cake or a pie or anything."

Kjersten giggled some more. Esther started laughing, too. And then Mama started.

"What's so funny?" Anna demanded.

"If this were a baseball game," Esther said, "you'd be out on three strikes. This is the third pie you've made that no one got to eat."

Now Anna started laughing. "Three strikes or not, I'm not quitting," she said. "Someday I will make a pie, and we will all eat it!"

CHAPTER 17

Friends at Last

Anna arrived at the baseball field early. She was one of the first spectators to claim a seat, so she made herself comfortable on the wooden bench along the first-base line. She arranged her blue calico dress so that it fell evenly around her knees and ankles and tucked in her shawl so it would not flap in the breeze. Her hair, braided carefully that morning, featured matching white ribbon bows.

Anna leaned forward to study the activities of the players. The Spitfires were warming up on the field, while the Oak Lake Boaters were having batting practice.

Gradually, more people came to watch the game. A few parents settled themselves on benches or quilts in the grass. Many of the spectators were brothers and sisters of the players.

Out of the corner of her eye, Anna saw Martha Wilkerson strolling across the field. Alice was with her. Anna turned her head to watch them more closely. Usually Martha and Alice and Edith came to baseball games with Samantha Landers. Samantha came to watch her brother, Tommy. But Samantha was not with Martha today.

Martha tossed her hair haughtily as she approached Anna. The bench was empty except for Anna, who sat perched at one end, but Martha and Alice did not pause.

"Hello, Martha. Hello, Alice," Anna said in her sweetest voice. "It's a fine day for a game, don't you think?"

Martha rolled her eyes. "I suppose." She kept walking right past Anna. Without speaking to Anna, Alice followed Martha to a patch of grass behind first base. There they put their heads together and giggled.

Anna was determined not to be annoyed. She turned her attention back to the field.

Richard fielded a ball Abe had tossed toward him. In one smooth motion, Richard scooped it out of the dirt, twisted, and snapped the ball to Jack, waiting on first base. Jack grinned and delivered the ball to Zachary on the pitcher's mound.

Abe signaled that the team should gather around second base. With his arms around the shoulders of Richard and Louis, Abe smiled proudly at all the Spitfires.

"You boys have been working very hard," Abe said. "In a few minutes, all your hard work is going to pay off."

"That's right," Elton said. "The Oak Lake Boaters will not even know what hit them."

"Zachary and Jack," Abe said, "do you remember the play we went over?"

Zach nodded enthusiastically. "If I see a runner taking a lead off of first base, I fire at Jack."

"And I keep my foot on the base so I'm always ready," Jack added. "We won't let any base runners get past us."

"Tony and Richard, are you ready for the double play balls?" Abe asked.

"Better than ever," Richard answered.

"And you've all been working on your swings. Keep your eye on the ball and stay steady."

Henry and Elton practiced swinging imaginary bats.

"Hey," Henry said, "where's Tommy? We need him to help cover the outfield."

The whole team turned to scan the playing field.

"There he is," Louis called out, pointing at left field.

Tommy was trotting across the field. Samantha was dragging behind him.

"Sorry I'm late," Tommy called out.

"We're just glad you're here," Jack said. "We need everybody today."

"Let's play ball!" Abe said, clapping his hands. The team scattered to take their positions.

Samantha hurried to get out of the way of the players. She shuffled across the infield toward the first-base line.

"Hi, Samantha!" Anna called out. "Come sit with me."

Martha and Alice burst into laughter. "Of course she's not going to sit with you," Martha said. "What made you think such a thing? Come on, Samantha, there's plenty of room for you over here."

Anna paid no attention to Martha. She kept her eyes fixed on Samantha, whose steps were slowing down.

"I'd like to hear about your aunt's engagement party," Anna said. "I'm sure everyone loved the dress you wore."

Samantha hesitated for just a moment. Then she turned her steps toward Anna. She came and sat on the bench. In the background, Martha gasped.

"Don't pay any attention to her," Anna advised.

"I won't," Samantha said. "I should have stopped following Martha Wilkerson around a long time ago."

"How was the engagement party?"

"It was nice. There were lots of sweet cakes and punch. But I kept wishing I was at Kjersten's birthday party."

"Really and truly?"

"Really and truly. You're right about Kjersten. She's nice. I like her. I'm sorry for making fun of her."

"She'll be glad to hear that," Anna said. "She's supposed to meet me here later."

Samantha turned her eyes to the field. "It looks like the game is about to start."

Zachary was studying the batter. With his left arm, he leaned on his knee. His right arm, with the ball in his hand, was tucked behind his back. Finally, he stood up straight, wound up, and threw the first pitch of the game.

It was a strike, straight and true. The batter swung and missed. The ball smacked into the hands of Leland, the catcher. With a whoop, Leland threw the ball back to Zach.

From the sideline, Abe caught Zach's eye. Zach nodded to indicate he had understood Abe's secret message. Zach got ready for the next pitch. The batter swung again, scraping the top of the ball with his bat and sending it dribbling into the infield. Richard easily stopped the rolling ball and threw it to Jack before the batter could get to first base.

Abe paced along the sideline, clapping his hands. "That's the way to do it, boys!"

"It looks like they're off to a good start," Samantha commented. "Tommy was a little worried on the way over here."

"That's because they lost so badly the last time," Anna said. "Zach wasn't here to hurl. But with Zach pitching and Jack Hammond playing first base, the other team doesn't have a chance."

Samantha smiled. "I hope you're right. But it's only the first inning."

"Go Spitfires!" Anna shouted.

"Beat the Boaters!" screamed a voice just behind her. Anna turned to see Martha Wilkerson standing behind the bench. Anna stared up at Martha with questions in her eyes.

"The ground is cold," Martha said. "You said there was plenty of room on the bench."

"There still is."

Samantha scooted closer to Anna. Martha and Alice sat down.

"If you're going to sit here," Samantha said, "you have to promise not to be mean."

Martha tilted her head, puzzled.

"I don't want you saying anything nasty about Kjersten or Anna or anybody."

Martha hardly knew what to say. "I promise," she finally said.

"Here comes Kjersten!" Anna said excitedly. "We have room on the bench for one more, don't we?"

"Certainly!" Samantha responded.

Kjersten's steps slowed as she approached the first-base line. Now she stopped. She caught Anna's eyes with her own worried ones.

Anna waved to Kjersten. "It's all right, Kjersten. Come and sit with us."

Kjersten did not move.

"What's the matter with her?" Martha asked.

Samantha scowled. "Would you want to come and sit with people who have been as mean to you as you've been to her?"

Martha hung her head. "No, I guess not."

Biting her lower lip, Kjersten looked from Anna to Samantha to Martha. She still did not move her feet.

Anna waved her arm in a big circle. "Come on, Kjersten. Come and sit."

Still Kjersten did not move.

136

Samantha stood up. "I'm going to get her."

Anna grinned and watched. Samantha marched over to Kjersten and took the Swedish girl by the hand. She pulled so hard that Kjersten had no choice but to follow. Samantha led Kjersten to the bench and pointed to the open spot between Martha and Alice. Gingerly, Kjersten sat down. She looked around nervously.

"It's all right," Samantha said. "We want to be your friends."

"Friends?"

"Yes, friends, just like Anna is your friend."

"Anna is friend."

"Yes, Anna is your friend. And so am I."

Kjersten smiled nervously. Samantha glared at Martha and Alice.

Awkwardly, Martha leaned over and put a hand on Kjersten's shoulder. "Sit with us whenever you want to. We're glad to have you."

Confused, Kjersten turned to Anna for reassurance.

Anna was smiling so big she could hardly talk. "It's all right, Kjersten. It's not a trick. We all want you to sit with us, to be our friend."

The crack of a bat made them turn their heads back to the game. The ball sailed to center field. Tommy Landers was under it and snatched it out of the air.

CHAPTER 18

Peace in the Family

Esther twirled to make her pink dress spin. "Do you like my pretty dress, Papa?" she asked.

"You look spectacular," Papa answered. He sat on the sofa in the living room. Anna was next to him, and Richard was in the chair across from him.

"I didn't get to wear my new Easter dress to Aunt Tina's for Easter dinner, so I decided to wear it today."

"You made a good choice," Papa said approvingly.

Anna watched Esther's spinning dress and thought of her own new sapphire cloak. It had not survived the Easter Sunday riot as well as Esther's dress had. She only got to wear the new cloak one day. Then it was so tattered that it went straight to the rag pile. Still, Anna was happy that Esther was enjoying her new dress.

"Are Uncle Enoch and Uncle Charles going to argue?" Esther asked somberly. "Are they going to shout and be mad like they were when they were here?"

Papa pulled Esther onto his knee. "I can't promise you what anyone will do. But I do think Charles and Enoch are trying to get along better these days."

"The strike is over, so they don't have to fight about that," Esther said bluntly.

Papa nodded.

"Teddy says that his papa quarrels with Uncle Enoch all the time."

"I don't think they quarrel all the time," Papa said slowly. "They do have different opinions about many things."

"But they can get along if they want to," Richard said. "Look at Jack and Zachary. A couple weeks ago they were so angry they were hitting each other. But now they get along again."

"And Martha and Kjersten are starting to be friends," Anna added. "Martha thinks Kjersten is really smart. Once she stopped making fun of her, she found out how much she likes Kjersten."

"And Enoch and Charles like each other, too," Papa said. "I'm sure of that. They've known each other for a long time."

"I'm glad we're going to have a family dinner," Esther said, "to make up for Easter."

Mama entered the room.

"Anna, your pie is ready to come out of the oven. As soon as you wrap it up, we can be on our way to the Stevensons'."

Richard snickered. "Are we going to get to eat this pie, Anna?"

"This pie is perfect," Anna declared. "I was very careful with the recipe."

A few minutes later, the Allerton family was walking down the street, laden with their part of the family dinner. Anna, of course, carried her cherry pie carefully and proudly. It was wrapped in two towels to keep it extra safe. Esther swung a basket of biscuits, Richard lugged a sack of potatoes, Papa had the corn pudding, and Mama had the apple pie.

"Are we going to ride a streetcar?" Esther asked.

"Here comes one now," Anna said.

"It's Mr. Hammond's car," Richard added. He waved his arm to signal that the car should stop for them.

They clambered aboard and settled into seats right behind Mr. Hammond.

"Jack tells me you hit quite a long ball against the Oak Lake team," Mr. Hammond said as he nudged the horses forward again.

Richard smiled proudly. "It was a triple. Two runs scored on my hit."

"I wish I could have been there," Mr. Hammond said. "Maybe I'll get to the next game."

"The season is just starting," Richard said. "We have all summer to play."

"Why are you carrying around half of a market?" Mr. Hammond asked, eyeing their food.

"We're going to have Easter dinner," Esther explained.

Mr. Hammond chuckled. "Well, that's a fine idea. There was quite a bit of excitement that day, wasn't there?"

"We're going to the Stevensons'," Esther said.

"Ah, yes, the coach's house. Jack is very excited to have Abe coaching."

They got off the streetcar in front of the Stevensons' house. Esther scampered up the steps and knocked on the door ahead of the rest of them. When it opened, she hurtled through, calling for Teddy.

Aunt Tina stood in the open doorway with Aunt Alison right behind her. They both laughed at Esther. Mama shook her head.

"When she gets excited," Mama said, "there's just nothing I can do to control her."

"Is everyone here?" Anna asked.

Aunt Tina nodded. "Polly and Judith are upstairs. No doubt they're talking about their latest beaus. Abe and Walter are out back in Abe's old lab."

"What about Uncle Enoch—and Uncle Charles?" Anna was almost too nervous to ask.

"Hmm," Aunt Tina said, puzzled. "I'm not sure where they disappeared to."

"These potatoes are heavy," Richard complained.

Aunt Tina took them from him. "Let's put the food in the kitchen. Anna, your pie smells delicious. I can't wait to taste it."

Anna and Mama followed Aunt Tina into the kitchen, where Aunt Alison was stirring her currant glaze in a pan on top of the stove. She smiled to welcome them.

"The ham smells wonderful!" Anna said as she set her pie down on the table and began unwrapping it.

Aunt Alison bent over and peeked at the ham in the oven. "It will be done in just a few minutes."

"I'll start peeling potatoes," Mama said, taking the sack from Aunt Tina.

"Alison," Aunt Tina said, "do you know what happened to Charles?"

"He was headed for the study the last time I saw him," Aunt Alison replied.

Aunt Tina raised her eyebrows. "Enoch's study?"

"Yes."

"Enoch was in there reading the last time I saw him."

Mama and Anna exchanged a worried glance.

Aunt Tina read their minds. "Perhaps I'll just go check and see how things are in the study."

"I'll go with you," Anna said.

As they approached the open study door, they heard rising voices.

"What on earth made you think to do such a thing?" Uncle Charles exclaimed.

"I'm simply using the mind that God gave me," Uncle Enoch answered adamantly. "I suggest you do the same."

"Oh, no!" Anna said. By now, Mama and Aunt Alison had heard the voices and followed them into the hallway. Papa and Richard left the living room and joined the growing huddle in the hall.

"Should we go in?" Mama asked.

"They have to work things out themselves," Aunt Tina insisted.

"They may need a little help," Papa said. He stepped toward the doorway. Immediately he tilted his head back and roared with laughter.

"Papa, what is it?" Anna asked anxiously.

Papa gestured that they should all come in. The two men sat across the desk from each other. Between them was a chess board. Most of the white pieces had been captured, and the king was checkmated. Uncle Enoch had the smirk of victory on his face.

"We haven't been playing more than ten minutes," Uncle Charles complained, "and already he's thrashed me."

Anna laughed in relief.

Uncle Charles pointed a finger at his brother-in-law. "This is not the end of it, my friend. I learn from my mistakes. You will not win so easily the next time."

"We all learn from our mistakes," Uncle Enoch said quietly. "Let us pray that the city of Minneapolis—even the whole country—can learn from its mistakes."

Uncle Charles nodded. "This nation has too much potential not to learn from its mistakes. If Jim Hill can build a railroad that reaches all the way to the West Coast, the rest of us can learn to solve our problems together."

Uncle Enoch chuckled. "May I remind you that Jim Hill has not reached the West Coast yet?"

Uncle Charles grinned in response. "It won't be long, now."

Anna caught Richard's eye and saw the smile on his dark face. The two men were bantering the way they always did. But the lightness in their tone and the twinkle in their eyes made everyone relax.

"I'd better get back to the potatoes," Mama said.

"Oh, the glaze is probably boiling by now," Aunt Alison said.

"Anna, I'm saving room for a piece of your pie," Uncle Charles said.

Anna smiled. "I'm afraid it's only one pie. It's not enough for fourteen people." She turned and headed for the kitchen.

"Well, I'm having a piece," Richard declared. "After all, you've made four pies and we haven't gotten to eat any of them yet."

"This pie made it all the way over here, safe and sound." Anna pushed open the kitchen door. "As soon as dinner's over—"

White-faced, Anna spun around and gasped at Richard.

"What is it?" Richard pushed past his sister and burst into the kitchen.

Teddy and Esther sat at the table with cherries smeared on their faces and soiled forks in their hands.

"We were hungry," Teddy explained.

Anna was too shocked to speak. Her beautiful pie was half-eaten. The remaining half was so crumbled that no one would want to eat it.

Richard roared with laughter. "I guess I'll have to wait for pie number five!"

There's More!

The American Adventure continues with *Chicago World's Fair*. Esther Allerton and her cousin Ted Fisk are going to the World's Fair in Chicago. They're excited to see Thomas Edison's new inventions. They ride on the new Ferris wheel and even get to talk on the phone to relatives who live back in Boston.

But there's no escaping the problems they know their friends are having. Across the country, banks are closing and railroads are going bankrupt. Thousands of people are losing their jobs, and families are going hungry. When Ted and Esther return to Minneapolis, a huge fire puts thousands more men out of work. Suddenly, Ted and Esther think of something they can do to help. Will it work?